"There's no easy way for me to say this, so I'll just put it straight out. I believe my wife gave birth to the little girl you adopted."

The words came at Sophie in slow motion, as if they'd been delivered from miles away. She dropped into the chair, her legs suddenly unable to support her. "What did you say?"

Caleb pulled a photo from his pocket and handed it to her.

She stared at it, leaden fear settling in her stomach. The picture had obviously been taken years ago, but the child captured there could have been Grace.

"I made an awful mistake," he said, "and gave her away."

The words hung there between them. In that moment, it happened, the thing Sophie had feared most since the day she'd received the incredible gift of her daughter. And her world blew apart into a million tiny pieces.

Dear Reader,

I think one of the more difficult realities of life to accept is that bad things happen to good people. It is decidedly sobering to see someone we know or love go through a tragedy that completely changes the course of his or her life.

The question we cannot help asking is why.

As I get older, I realize that sometimes there isn't any apparent or acceptable answer.

I've known people who have been dealt unbelievable blows, the kind of senseless violence or loss that would justify a complete withdrawal from a world that can prove too cruel. But in some of these same people I've witnessed a strength of character, an unwillingness to give up that has been an inspiration to me, made me look for the rainbow in circumstances that might at first glance seem hopeless.

In *A Gift of Grace* I'm hoping that you'll find Caleb and Sophie to be two such people—a man and woman who manage to get back on their feet when accepting that their lives are essentially over would be a reasonable option.

Both Caleb and Sophie face a turning point where they must decide what the rest of their lives will be and whether they have the courage to accept the gift that awaits them.

Please visit my Web site at www.inglathcooper.com for a look at my other titles. I'd love to hear from you at P.O. Box 973, Rocky Mount, VA 24151 or inglathc@aol.com.

All best,

Inglath Cooper

Books by Inglath Cooper

HARLEQUIN SUPERROMANCE

For my mother, Margie McGuire, whose strength of spirit and ability to find the good in the difficult are an inspiration to me. And, too, for teaching me the things that matter.

A GIFT OF GRACE
Inglath Cooper

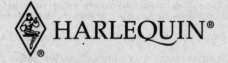

HARLEQUIN®

TORONTO • NEW YORK • LONDON
AMSTERDAM • PARIS • SYDNEY • HAMBURG
STOCKHOLM • ATHENS • TOKYO • MILAN • MADRID
PRAGUE • WARSAW • BUDAPEST • AUCKLAND

ISBN 0-373-71352-5

A GIFT OF GRACE

Copyright © 2006 by Inglath Cooper.

All rights reserved. Except for use in any review, the reproduction or utilization of this work in whole or in part in any form by any electronic, mechanical or other means, now known or hereafter invented, including xerography, photocopying and recording, or in any information storage or retrieval system, is forbidden without the written permission of the publisher, Harlequin Enterprises Limited, 225 Duncan Mill Road, Don Mills, Ontario, Canada M3B 3K9.

All characters in this book have no existence outside the imagination of the author and have no relation whatsoever to anyone bearing the same name or names. They are not even distantly inspired by any individual known or unknown to the author, and all incidents are pure invention.

This edition published by arrangement with Harlequin Books S.A.

® and TM are trademarks of the publisher. Trademarks indicated with ® are registered in the United States Patent and Trademark Office, the Canadian Trade Marks Office and in other countries.

www.eHarlequin.com

Printed in U.S.A.

PROLOGUE

CALEB TUCKER'S WIFE DIED on one of the prettiest days ever lent to Albemarle County.

Channel eight's morning weather anchor had declared it the pearl in the oyster of spring—get out and enjoy it, folks!—but to Caleb, the beauty of the day was simply another irony in the nightmare that had taken over his life.

He sat on a chair by the metal-railed hospital bed, his skin chilled by air-conditioning lowered to a level more appropriate for preservation than comfort. He wondered how many other people before him had sat here in this same spot, not willing to let go. In the past eight months, he had come to hate this chair, this room, as if they alone were responsible for the misery now etched into every cell of his body.

He clutched his wife's hand between his own, the backs of his knuckles whitened, his grip too tight, too desperate.

A half hour ago, two somber doctors had

walked into the room where he'd sat waiting, both his parents and Laney's parents hovering behind him. He'd watched their mouths move, the words sitting on the surface of comprehension. "We're sorry, Mr. Tucker. We were forced to perform an emergency cesarean. There were complications from the anesthesia. I'm afraid she's gone."

No. Not possible. Not after everything she'd been through. She was going to get better. She *had* to get better.

He'd asked to see her, alone, trying to block out the sounds of Mary Scott's keening grief. The doctors had led him to the room, one on either side of him, as if they thought he might not make it without their help.

He had only wanted them to go away, leave him alone with her.

Once they'd closed the door behind them, he'd stood staring at her beautiful face, seen nothing there to hint at the life she had carried inside her these past months. Nothing to hint at the act of violence responsible for that life. She'd looked peaceful, accepting, unmarked by any memory of what had happened, peace erasing all traces of pain or fear.

For that, he was grateful.

It was all he could find to be grateful for now.

The day had arrived after months of dread, of

willing time to slow, praying for God to bring her back to him. But Laney—the woman he had loved since he was sixteen years old—was no longer here.

The door to the room opened and hit the wall with a bang. Mary Scott stood in the entrance, her face haggard. She looked as if she had aged a dozen years in the past few hours. Behind her, Laney's father, Emmitt Scott, put a restraining hand on her shoulder.

"Mary, come on," he said. "Don't do this."

She stared at Caleb now, her eyes glazed with blame. "This is your fault," she said, her voice ragged, high-pitched. "Because of you, my daughter is dead."

Caleb let the words settle, the knife of accusation stabbing through his chest.

"If you had been the kind of husband she had wanted you to be, none of this would ever have happened. Do you know how many times she came home crying to me about the two of you never seeing each other? About work coming before everything else, including her?"

The last few words rang out on the edge of hysteria.

"Mary, stop now," Emmitt Scott said, taking his wife's arm.

But she jerked away, crossed the floor in a

couple of strides and slapped Caleb hard across the face.

He sat, too numb to register more than a momentary flash of pain, and then gratitude flooded him for the realization that he could feel anything at all.

Mary glanced at her hand, then back at him.

"Mary!" Emmitt swung her up in his arms, his face taut. "I'm sorry, Caleb. We'll come back when you're done," he said and carried her from the room.

Caleb stared at the door long after it had closed. No matter how much Mary blamed him, it could never equal the blame he had leveled at himself. He dropped his head onto the icy bed rail, grief swallowing him, the sounds coming from deep inside nearly inhuman. No tears, though. He'd never shed one. Not since the police had found her broken body behind a Dumpster twenty miles from the mall where her car had been left with the driver's door open, the contents of her purse spilled onto the pavement below.

A thousand times he had asked himself why he hadn't driven with her that night. One decision made under the carelessly arrogant assumption that they would have other nights, other opportunities. "Come on, Caleb, you can fix the tractor in the morning." He heard her voice as clear as if it were yesterday. "We'll just go buy Mama's birthday present and then eat at that new Italian place I was telling you about. When was the last time we went out to dinner?"

"I can't, honey," he'd said. "I need to get it going so I can get hay off the ground tomorrow. We'll go this weekend, okay?"

One small flicker of disappointment in her blue eyes, and then Laney had smiled, as she always had. Forgiven him, as she always had.

She had gone on without him, kissing him on the mouth when she'd left, telling him he worked too hard. She'd be back soon.

And he'd taken that for granted. Because of course she would be back. That was how life worked, wasn't it? One day blending seamlessly into the next until a man never thought to question his right to it.

He leaned forward, pressed his lips to the back of his wife's wrist, stung by its increasing coolness. Despite all the words he'd heard countless times from doctors renowned for their expertise in brain-damaged patients, he had continued to hope that this moment would never actually happen, that she would wake up, come back to him. "Laney," he whispered. "Oh, dear God, I'm so sorry."

Footsteps on the tile floor echoed, penetrating his consciousness far enough to prompt him to raise his head.

Dr. Richards stood at the foot of the bed, his short dark hair disheveled, as if he'd been running his hands through it. He cleared his throat. "Mr. Tucker." The pause held a note of hopefulness. "Are you sure you don't want to see the baby? It might make a difference."

Caleb stared at him, as if the man had spoken a language Caleb didn't understand. "Call the agency," he said.

For a brief moment, the doctor's composure slipped, and under a burdened sigh, he said, "If you're sure then."

"I'm sure."

CHAPTER ONE

Three years later

SOPHIE OWENS PULLED the last clean plate from the dishwasher and placed it in the cabinet by the sink. The dinner dishes were done, the kitchen back in order for the next morning.

Norah Jones drifted down from the speakers mounted in the ceiling of the house's main living areas. For a long time after her divorce, Sophie's need for music had been about cloaking her own loneliness in whatever flavor of song seemed most likely to lift and soothe. Now, it felt more like an old friend whose company she simply enjoyed.

Wiping her hands on a dish towel, Sophie wandered into the living room, where her daughter sat in the middle of the floor surrounded by a ramshackle collection of LEGO toys.

This was the largest room in the house, with a stretch of wide windows on the front and a fieldstone fireplace at one end. Two oversize Bernhardt chairs sat on either side of its opening, a leather sofa the color of cognac closer to the center of the room. An antique rug covered most of the floor, its primary role a playground for Grace.

The house wasn't huge, but comfortable in a way that made Sophie glad she had taken the plunge two years ago and bought it. To a girl from southwest Virginia, Charlottesville real estate was expensive. On an English professor's salary, it had been an enormous debt, but so worth it with its fenced yard and proximity to the university.

And, too, the neighborhood was the sort where Grace already had friends who lived close by, who would no doubt in years to come ride over on their bicycles, have pajama parties in the attic. Hard to imagine Grace being old enough to do such things, but she was almost three, and these first years had flown by.

"Time for your bath, sweet pea," Sophie said.

Grace looked up, her wide blue eyes the focal point of a round, rosy-cheeked face so beautiful that people often stared at her. "And then you'll read me my story?"

"I will," Sophie promised. She looked forward to their nightly bath-time ritual almost as much as Grace. Grace loved water, had taken to it as if it were as natural to her as air.

A few minutes later, Grace sat in the tub, eyes

lit with happiness. She slapped both palms against the bubble-filled water, sending a poof of suds up to land on Sophie's chin. She squealed with laughter. "Mama has a beard!" she said.

Sophie laughed, scooped up a dollop of soapy bubbles and gave Grace one, too, inciting another round of giggles.

Finally, when they were both soaked, Sophie lifted Grace from the tub, wrapping her in a thick white towel and dressing her in the Winnie-the-Pooh pajamas that were her favorite.

Sophie carried her into the bedroom. Stuffed animals covered a toddler-size sleigh bed. Grace couldn't bring herself to banish any of them to the floor.

In this room, Sophie could be accused of over-indulgence, the walls a color-washed pink and yellow she had done herself. Grace said it looked like the sunrise. An old school desk sat in one corner with a stack of coloring books and crayons. A hand-hooked rug with Curious George at its center covered the floor.

"Where's Blanky?" Grace asked as she snuggled up under the covers.

"He had a bath today, too," Sophie said. "I forgot to get him out of the drier. Be right back."

In the laundry room, Sophie retrieved the shabby but well-loved once-pink blanket. This was another subject she should probably tackle, but Grace's attachment to it was so complete that Sophie couldn't bring herself to take it away from her. She figured it would resolve itself eventually. She'd yet to see any of her freshman English students dragging Blankys into the classroom.

At Sophie's return, Grace smiled and tucked the blanket under her left arm, resting her chin on its threadbare silk edging.

"Which book do we get to read tonight, Mama?"

"Which one would you like?"

"Are You My Mother?"

They'd read the Dr. Seuss book countless times, and Grace never tired of it. At one point, Sophie had begun to worry that on some level Grace felt the question within herself. She had never explained to Grace how she had come to be her daughter. It wasn't something Sophie meant to hide from her. She had just never been able to say the words for fear that they would dissolve even an ounce of her daughter's security.

Some days when Sophie caught sight of her child, framed in one of her high, sweet giggles, gratitude nearly brought her to her knees. She had lived the first year of Grace's life in terror that it couldn't last. That terror had quieted, but never completely gone away. It didn't seem possible that anyone could give up a gift so precious as this and not realize their mistake.

But the days had turned to weeks, then months. Had it really been three years since the agency social worker had placed the newborn infant in her arms? Sophie could not remember what her days had been like without Grace. Only that life now had a buzz, a rhythm to it that made her previous existence seem that and only that. Existing.

Soon then. She would explain things to her daughter soon. She didn't want to wait until Grace was old enough to think Sophie had intentionally hidden the truth from her.

She pulled the book from the shelf, sat down on the bed and, putting one arm around her daughter, began to read. Grace's chin quivered. Tears slid down her cheeks as the little bird went from kitten to cow to dog searching for its mother.

By the time the bird finally found her, Grace's tense shoulders relaxed, her eyes heavy with sleep. Sophie closed the book, kissed her daughter's forehead. "Sweet dreams. Say your prayers?"

Grace nodded, reciting the verse she repeated each night before going to sleep. Sophie tucked the covers around her and smoothed a hand across her daughter's silky hair.

"Good night." She flicked off the lamp and turned to leave.

"Mama?"

"Yes, baby?"

"I'm glad you're my mommy."

Tears welled in Sophie's eyes. "Me, too, sweetie. Me, too."

CALEB TUCKER SAT on the front porch of the old farmhouse his grandparents had built in 1902. On the floor next to him lay Noah, a yellow Labrador retriever so named for his avoidance of water as a puppy; even rain puddles had sent him flying back to the nearest pair of available arms.

Surrounding the house were four hundred acres of farmland, the soil rich and dark with three generations of nurturing. Pockets of woods thick with century-old oak and maple trees divided hay fields from pasture. Deer slipped into the alfalfa fields just before sunset every evening. Flocks of wild turkeys pecked their way from one end of the farm to the other and back again in an endless loop of foraging.

The land had been in Caleb's father's family for three generations, the kind of acreage that in this part of Virginia now required the bank account of a stock-market genius or some thirty-year-old Internet wizard to afford.

The permanence of the land and its need of him held Caleb back from the brink of something too awful to define.

The moon had just started its ascent from behind Craig Mountain. It was full tonight, the pastures east of the house bathed in soft light, the Black Angus cows grazing there clearly outlined.

The day had been long, and Caleb had worked his muscles just short of failure. It was how he ended every day, wrung out, collapsing into the wicker chair and forfeiting dinner in exchange for a Dr Pepper and some cheese crackers, most of which stayed in the pack.

Headlights arced up the gravel drive, his dad's old Ford truck rumbling over the knoll just short of the house. Caleb's parents lived on the other end of the farm in a house they had built ten years ago. Jeb Tucker stopped and got out, balancing a plate covered in Saran wrap.

An older version of his only son, his hair had gone steel gray before Caleb had left home for college. Jeb had passed along the defined bone structure of his face as well as his wide, full mouth. Both father and son were heavily muscled from the daily routine of farm life. Like Jeb, Caleb favored Wranglers and Ropers. Dressy for both of them meant putting on their newest pair.

He looked up at Caleb now, his jaw set. "Evenin'," he said.

"Dad." Caleb nodded. Noah thumped his tail on the porch floor in greeting.

"Your mother asked me to bring this over," Jeb said.

"You didn't have to do that."

"She thinks you're not eating."

"Tell her I'm fine."

"Maybe you ought to tell her. She doesn't listen to me too much anymore." Jeb set the plate on the step, then lowered himself down beside it.

Caleb didn't miss the note of resignation in his father's voice, and he realized how long it had been since he'd asked how they were doing. "You two okay?"

Jeb looked out across the darkened yard. "No," he said. "I can't say we are."

Caleb let that settle and then asked, "This about me?"

Jeb looked down at the step, traced a pattern across the wood and answered without looking up. "It's about the fact that none of us has moved on—"

Caleb erupted from his chair, his back to his father. "Don't do this, Dad."

"Don't you think it's about time we talked about it, son?"

"About what?" Caleb snapped back, swinging around. "The fact that I miss my wife so much that sometimes I feel like I can't breathe for the pain of it?"

Jeb shook his head. "I know you miss her, Caleb. God knows we all do. But the fact is you haven't moved a step beyond the day she died. It's like quicksand, and it's pulling you down. It's pulling us all down."

"That's not fair, Dad."

"There's not a damn thing about any of this that's fair, Caleb," Jeb said, anger in his voice now. "But you are still here. Still alive. Somehow, some way, you have got to move on."

"And what does that mean?" Caleb asked, forcing a level note to his voice. "Finding somebody else?"

"Maybe," Jeb said quietly. "Don't you think that's what she would want?"

"I think she wanted the two of us to have a family, raise our kids, spoil our grandkids and grow old together. Those are the things I know she wanted."

Jeb started to say something, stopped, pressed his lips together, and then said, "That's what we all wanted for the two of you."

"Yeah, well, we didn't get that, did we?"

"No, son. You didn't." He stared up at Caleb. "You're a young man. You can still have a good life with someone."

"Don't!" Caleb said. "Just don't, okay?"

A few moments of silence ticked past before Jeb stood, rubbing the back of his neck with one hand. "We're going down to your aunt Betsy's for the weekend. You can get us on the cell phone if you need us."

Caleb watched as his dad got in the truck and drove off, standing in the same spot long after the taillights had disappeared down the drive. The moon slipped higher in the sky. An owl hooted in a nearby tree, the sound stirring inside him a fresh swirl of loneliness.

He flipped on the radio he kept on the porch for company. Static crackled in the air before the dial came into focus. He could only pick up the AM station out of D.C. after dark.

Vivaldi's Spring Concerto rose high and tender from the old radio. This music had been Laney's. His only by association. She had thought it beautiful. To him, it had sounded like a foreign language, noise that he didn't understand. But he found himself reaching for it now, his connection to her thinning like a frayed rope. The music was a medium through which he could still feel her, remember what it had been like to make love to her, her skin soft beneath his hands.

He closed his eyes, leaned his head against the wicker rocker. He didn't listen every night. He couldn't. Only when he needed the music's poignant emotion to remind him he could still feel. Because even if all he felt was sadness, at least that was something.

He tried to focus on the picture he carried of her in his head, alarmed by its lack of clarity and the way it continued to dim like a photograph left too long in the light.

A soft breeze stirred, and his nostrils suddenly filled with the sweet scent of her perfume.

"Laney," he said, his voice a hoarse plea.

He felt her touch on his shoulders like the brush of a feather. He sat as still as stone, afraid a single movement would shatter the feeling like glass all around him. And then he heard it, the wrenching sound of her weeping.

His heart twisted, felt suddenly too large for his chest. Tears streamed from his own eyes. He didn't bother to wipe them away. "Laney," he said. "Laney."

CHAPTER TWO

JEB FOLLOWED THE GRAVEL ROAD that led back to the house he shared with his wife, the speedometer needle never reaching twenty. What was the point in hurrying?

There had been a time when he couldn't wait to get home every day. Couldn't wait to see Catherine. It had been that way all through Caleb's childhood. Even after Caleb had left home for college, Jeb and Catherine had known a renewal of sorts in their marriage. He'd come home some nights to find her at the door in a piece of lingerie that made his heart hit the wall of his chest, and they would make love on the kitchen's old walnut table.

Now, he couldn't even remember the last time they had touched each other.

He blinked hard as if he could shake the gray pall that reality settled over him. But it stayed where it was, so heavy there were times he thought he would simply disintegrate beneath it.

He loved his wife, but somewhere in these last three years, he had lost her.

He stopped the truck in the middle of the road, leaned forward with his forearms on the steering wheel, staring up at the night sky. If he could just turn the clock back, figure out how to have what they'd once had. He'd tried to talk Catherine into seeing someone, even both of them together, but she wouldn't hear of it. She'd always been one to hold everything inside, a deal-with-it-herself kind of person. Only this was too big, too much. For either of them. And their marriage had bent to the will of their grief, of Caleb's grief.

With a weary heart, he straightened in the seat, pressed the accelerator on the crochety old truck and headed home.

ON THURSDAY MORNING, Sophie drove the short distance from her house to the University of Virginia campus with her window cracked, letting in the flavor of the crisp morning. Spring was her favorite season; she loved the trees with their newborn leaves, the tulips popping up from their winter nest. To Sophie, the world felt more hopeful at this time of year, as if all things were possible.

She stopped at Starbucks for her morning fix, then got back in the Volvo and turned the radio to NPR, only half listening to Terry Gross interview a newly published author. Her thoughts were on the day ahead and the details left to tie up for Grace's birthday party. After her first class, Sophie planned to pick Grace up from day care and run a few errands, things she wouldn't have time to do tomorrow.

Her cell phone rang just as she pulled into the faculty parking lot.

She glanced at caller ID, ran a hand through her hair and suppressed a groan. She could ignore it, but that would only prolong the inevitable.

With a sigh, she hit the talk button. "Hi, Aunt Ruby."

"My goodness, you actually answered," was the dry reply.

"What's up?" Sophie said, ignoring the barb behind the greeting.

"Do I need a reason to call and see how you're doing?" she asked, her voice hoarse with forty years' worth of cigarettes. "We haven't heard from you in months. I thought something might be wrong."

"Everything's fine," Sophie said, not adding that it was these conversations that usually sent a perfectly fine day flying right off track.

"How's little Grace?"

"She's great."

"About to turn three, isn't she?"

"Yes, difficult as it is to believe."

"Are you doing a party for her?"

"Nothing elaborate," Sophie hedged.

"Oh." Ruby paused and then said, "I assume we aren't invited."

"Aunt Ruby, it's not that kind of thing. Just a few of her friends from preschool—"

"Are you ashamed of us, Sophie?" she interrupted. "After everything we did for you?"

Sophie let several beats of silence pass, reaching for calm. "Of course not."

"What else am I supposed to think?" Ruby said, her voice threaded with quiet hurt.

Sophie started to protest, to say once and for all that she'd had enough of her aunt's guilt trips, but stopped herself just short of it as she always did. Because Ruby was right about one thing. She and Uncle Roy had taken Sophie in when she'd had no one else in the world, and the only other option for her would have been a foster home.

"It's not a big deal, Aunt Ruby. I didn't think you'd want to come. That's all."

"You don't have to justify your actions to me, Sophie. I mean, we hardly know the child."

Sophie dropped her head against the seat, massaging one temple where a subtle headache had begun to throb. "You know you have an open invitation to visit anytime."

Another stretch of silence. "Then maybe we'll

drive up for the party and bring her a present. When is it?"

"Saturday afternoon at one," Sophie said with resignation.

"Nothing like advance notice," Ruby said, sarcasm coating the words. "Anyway, we'll be there. Don't want that little girl to grow up not even knowing who we are."

Sophie bit her lip to keep from reminding her aunt she had never once invited Grace and her for a visit. "I have a class to get to, Aunt Ruby. We'll see you on Saturday."

She clicked off the phone and then sat for a few moments thinking how odd the call had been, trying to remember the last time they had even talked. It wasn't like her aunt to call her out of the blue. With Ruby, there was always a catch. Sophie felt sure this time would not be an exception.

CALEB LIKED TO drive with his window rolled down; even on winter days, he'd turn the heater up full blast and let the outside in. This Thursday morning, he pulled into his parking space at the side entrance of Tucker Farm Supply, warm April sunshine pouring in. The store sat at the south end of Main Street in an old two-story brick building that had once been home to Miller Produce.

Jeb had bought the building and started the

business some twenty-five years ago, and Caleb had grown up working summers loading trucks and running the front register. It was a small business by most standards, but firmly rooted in the community with a following of loyal customers.

Caleb got out of the truck, Noah leaping down behind him, tail wagging. Inside the store, Noah did a quick survey for Russell, an overweight tabby whose job it was to patrol the building for trespassing mice. Noah glimpsed Russell's tail disappearing behind one of the display cases and spun out on the concrete floor.

The cat made it to the fescue seed barrel with seconds to spare, already cleaning his front paw with a touch of arrogance by the time Noah slid to a stop in front of him.

"Never gives up, does he?" Macy Stephens stood behind the old wood counter at the front of the store with a bottle of Pledge in one hand and a white cotton cleaning rag in the other. She spritzed the top of the counter, rubbing hard until the aged wood shone.

Caleb shook his head. "One of these days, he's gonna flatten some nice old lady who never saw him coming."

Macy smiled. "We all have our goals in life."

Caleb registered a hint of fresh-smelling perfume and the fact that Macy was wearing her hair down most days now instead of in the ponytail she used to keep it pulled back with. She had started working at the store part-time when she'd begun classes at the university. She was about to finish up this year and planned to teach elementary school in the fall.

"The Spring Festival starts this weekend." Macy added another squirt of furniture polish to the countertop, her gaze a few inches short of his.

Caleb stepped behind the counter and reached for the box of receipts beneath the register. "Mmm-hmm."

"Any interest in going?"

Normally, Caleb would have answered with an automatic no, but something in her face made him reach for a softer note. "Lotta work to do this weekend."

"Oh," she said, nodding.

"You going?"

"Thought I might."

"Sounds like good weather for it."

"Hope so."

"All right, then. I'll be upstairs taking a look at the month's statement."

"Okay," she said and turned her back to him.

In his office, Caleb pulled a chair up to the heavy oak desk by the window that looked out over the feed store's main floor. He worked for a couple of hours, glancing over receipts, comparing margins on certain labels of feed they sold, dog food, cat food, grain for horses. Tucker Farm Supply wasn't the kind of business that would ever make a man rich, but it was a comfortable living, a stable one. If there was anything Caleb appreciated now, it was stability. He clung to the things in his life that didn't change, weeded out what did.

The bell to the front door dinged several times while he worked, customers going in and out. It was almost noon when he stood and stretched just as the door jingled again. A woman came in with a little girl holding on to her hand. The child said something and the woman nodded. The little girl took off for the corner of the store, headed straight for the seed barrel where Noah and Russell were still maintaining their standoff.

The woman stepped to the counter, said something to Macy. The child squatted beside Noah, rubbing his head. Noah's attention, strangely enough, had been diverted from the cat. He sat with his nose in the air, his eyes closed in absolute appreciation of the child's doting.

Caleb turned away from the window, sat down at the desk a little too quickly so that the chair tipped back. The phone buzzed. "Yeah, Macy."

"Do you know if we've got any more of that hay in the shed out back?"

"Few bales, I think."

"Dr. Owens wants to buy some."

Caleb peered over the window again at the woman by the register. He didn't recall seeing her in the store before. "That'll be fine."

"Eddie left for lunch a few minutes ago. Think you could help load it?"

"Be right down."

He took the stairs two at a time, nodding at the woman as he passed the register and said, "Where you parked, ma'am?"

"In front," she said.

"Mind pulling around back?"

"No."

"It'll be the first white shed."

"Okay." She looked at Macy and added, "Is it all right if my daughter stays in here for a minute?"

"Of course. Noah's loving it. I'll keep an eye on her."

"Be right back then," the woman said, following Caleb out the door and then veering right to a dark blue Volvo station wagon parked near the front of the store.

Caleb opened the shed, flicked on the light and tossed out three bales of orchard grass hay just as the woman backed toward the building.

She got out of the car and smiled at him. "Oh, good. That's exactly what I needed."

Her smile was open and friendly, as if she used it often. He eyed the car and said, "How many did you want?"

"Four or five would be great, but—"

"Looks like two's about all that'll fit if you leave the tailgate open."

She worried a full lower lip with noticeably white teeth. "Oh. Well, I can come back for whatever doesn't. Except I have a class this afternoon. What time do you close?"

"Five o'clock," he said.

"I won't be able to get back by then. Maybe I can come in the morning?"

He glanced at his watch. "Where do you live?"

"Ivy Run Road."

"I could drop them off for you. I was headed out on an errand, anyway."

Her face brightened. "That would be great. We're having a birthday party, and I still have a thousand things to do—"

"No problem," he said. "Just give me the address."

"Actually, I have to run back by there on the way to school. Could you possibly go now?"

"Sure. I'll follow you over."

"Let me just run in and pay then."

Caleb nodded, tossing a couple more bales from

the shed while she pulled her Volvo out front. He backed his truck up, loaded the hay, then headed inside to tell Macy he would be gone an hour or so.

The woman and child stood by the register. Macy was looking at the little girl with that same odd expression on her face that he'd noticed when they'd first come in the store. The little girl clutched her mother's hand, talking nonstop about the yellow dog and the big cat. Something about her rang out like an echo inside him. He frowned, then glanced at the woman, who smiled expectantly and said, "I really appreciate this."

"No problem," he said. "I'll be right behind you."

Ten minutes later, they turned onto a paved driveway off tree-lined Ivy Run Road. Caleb backed in behind her. He got out and she met him at the truck. The little girl had already taken off around one side of the house.

"Do you think we could put those in the backyard?" she asked, raising her voice above the rumble of the truck's diesel engine.

"Sure," he said, popping the tailgate and grabbing a bale with each hand. "Just show me where."

She nodded and moved off in the direction the child had taken, saying again how much she appreciated his help.

The house was neat and well maintained, not huge, but cottagelike with groomed boxwoods neatly clipped into roundness. A huge old magnolia tree stood to one side of the lawn. At the rear of the house, Caleb came up short. The backyard looked as if FAO Schwarz had set up a display. Big red slide with a small trampoline-like thing at its base. A playhouse in bright yellow and green with shutters. A mini picnic table where two dolls sat waiting for tea. The little girl was at the top of the slide, getting ready to come down.

"Watch, Mommy!"

She turned to look, shading her eyes with one hand. "Be careful, honey."

The girl zipped down, hitting the trampoline at the bottom and letting out a high squeal-giggle that had delight at its center.

The woman stopped at the edge of the yard. "You can put that down here," she said, smiling at him. "I'll figure out where to place it later."

"I'd be glad to put it where you need it."

"Well, okay." One finger under her chin, she said, "I thought we could use them as chairs for the children. How about under the oak tree?"

Caleb nodded and dropped the bales. "I'll get the rest."

Two trips back to the truck, and the last of the

bales formed an L-shaped backless bench at the yard's perimeter.

"Thank you so much," she said. "We're having a barnyard party on Saturday. Mini-donkeys. Grace has hardly been able to sleep for thinking about it."

The little girl skipped over and took her mother's hand. "They're only a little taller than me," she said, looking up at Caleb.

"Perfect size then, huh?"

"I haven't even introduced myself," the woman said. "I'm Sophie Owens. And this is my daughter, Grace."

"Caleb Tucker."

"Oh." She tipped her head back, her eyes widening a fraction. "Then you own the—"

"My family does, yes."

"Well, again, thank you so much for hauling those out here for me."

"No problem."

"Is that your dog at the store?" the little girl asked.

"He is."

"I like him."

"I think he liked you, too." Caleb looked into the child's clear blue eyes. She smiled at him, a shy child's smile, and in that single moment, Caleb saw her. Dark arching eyebrows contrasting with sunshine-blond hair. The small square chin.

He took a near stumbling step backward, as if he'd been delivered a blow to the chest. Snapshot memories of Laney as a little girl flew through his mind. Not possible. A too-long stretch of silence dropped over them like a blanket trapping all available air beneath it.

"How old will you be, Grace?" he asked, his voice unsteady.

She held up three fingers. "This many."

Her birthday was Saturday. The twenty-second of April.

The day Laney's child had been born.

The day Laney had died.

CHAPTER THREE

HE WAS LOSING HIS MIND.

No other explanation for it. Things like this didn't happen. The world was too big a place.

When Caleb arrived back at the store, Macy stood at the front counter, sorting invoices.

She looked up, started to say something, then stopped. "Caleb, you look like you just saw a ghost. What's wrong?"

"Dr. Owens. Is she married?"

Macy closed the folder in front of her. "Divorced. I know a graduate student who helps out as a part-time nanny to her daughter. Ann Whitley. Really nice girl. She says Dr. Owens has inspired her to adopt a child some day."

The words hit Caleb at a decibel so high he thought he might have imagined them. The truth fluttered down, registered. He gave an abrupt nod, told Macy he had some work to do at the farm, then called Noah and got in the truck, heading home with little memory of how he'd gotten there.

In the driveway, he jumped out, loping into the house and up the stairs to the second floor. At the top and to the right was another smaller staircase that led to the attic. He opened the door, a whoosh of heat hitting him in the face. Sunlight cut through the dormer window on the far wall. Boxes covered the floor, lined the walls. All Laney's. He'd put everything that belonged to her in this room. Out of sight. Unable to throw any of it away, equally unable to look at it.

He hadn't opened this door once since the week after her funeral when he'd hauled it all up here. Box after box until he'd collapsed, exhausted, in the bed they had shared. He had slept for three days straight.

He weaved his way into the room and knocked over a tall box, spilling two of her competition swimsuits and a pair of goggles. He put them back where they'd been.

Most of the boxes were sealed and unmarked. He moved to the far wall, pulled out a couple of smaller ones, using his pocketknife to slit the tape. Inside was a quilt her grandmother had made her for college graduation. A half-full bottle of Chanel No. 5. A set of electric hot curlers. The next box held books and a headset she'd used for running.

He opened a half dozen more, dumping their contents onto the floor, reaching for another when he didn't find what he was looking for.

Finally. There.

A dozen or more framed photographs he'd pulled from their living-room walls three years before, pictures of them both as children, as high-school sweethearts, as husband and wife.

He lifted them out, one by one, each picture creating its own well of pain. He and Laney at junior-year homecoming, her hair long, blond and straight. He and Laney on the rocks at Badger Creek playing hooky from school. There were pictures of him as a boy, an elementary-school photo when he'd decided to give himself a crew cut with his dad's horse clippers.

And there were pictures of Laney. Prom queen. Preening with Alice and Amy, her two best friends from high school.

At the bottom of the stack was the one he'd been looking for. Laney as a toddler standing next to her father.

Caleb flipped the frame. On the back she had written: *Me and Daddy. Three years old. Me not him!*

He turned it over again, stared at the little girl in the picture. If he'd needed proof of the resemblance to the child he'd met today, here it was.

Same silky blond hair. Blue eyes with their long, dark lashes. Even the mouth was the same. Wide and full.

Caleb sat down on the wood floor, propped his head on one hand and stared at the picture.

How could this have happened?

His life had finally begun to even out, to settle into something he could accept as living. Now, all the old pain was back, rushing through his veins like injected poison.

He sat for a long time, his eyes closed, head against the wall behind him.

An extraordinary sense of calm slid over him, as it had the other times just before he sensed her presence.

He kept his eyes closed, knowing that if he opened them, she would slip away.

A single touch to the back of his hand, and he knew she was there. As she had been countless times in the past three years.

He wondered if these moments were the only thing that kept him going. Wondered if all this time he had been straddling the line between the sane and insane, if visits from a dead wife automatically put a person in that category.

He had told no one about it. Not his mom or dad. Not his doctor or pastor. As real as he knew her presence was, he could not bring himself to share it with anyone else for fear that maybe he really was going crazy.

He sat for a long time, the peace inside him the only proof he had that he wasn't losing his mind. It had been like this when she'd been alive, as well, Laney's ability to soothe, to bring reason and calm to the times in their lives completely void of either.

With the calm, the feel of her touch receded, and he was alone again. He opened his eyes then, stared up at the slow-twirling ceiling fan above him. Tears spilled down his cheeks and fell onto the glass covering her face.

CATHERINE TUCKER SAT in a striped lawn chair, enjoying the sun's warmth.

The backyard of Betsy Marshall's modest, but immaculate, North Carolina ranch-style home was full to overflowing. Jeb and his brother Saul were in charge of the grill. The smell of sizzling hamburgers and hot dogs threaded the late-spring breeze.

Jeb came from a large, extended family. The opposite of Catherine, who had been an only child. His sister Betsy was the third in a family of five children, and she was the most like Jeb's mother in that she loved to get the whole family together, seemed happiest in the middle of so much talking and laughing.

Jeb stood by the grill now, smiling at something his brother had said. He looked more relaxed than she had seen him in a long time. Unfair though it might have been, a wave of resentment washed up through her, made her face too warm, like the hot flashes she'd had after she'd stopped the hormone-replacement therapy a couple of years ago.

In that moment, she saw the two of them on either side of a huge divide, she still immersed in grief, he ready to move on. He wanted her to go with him. Catherine knew this. And yet it was as if her feet were planted in concrete. No matter how desperately she tried to pull herself free, she couldn't.

"You're awfully quiet."

Catherine glanced up. Betsy stood in front of her, holding two red cups. She handed one to Catherine. "Iced tea. Sweet like you like it."

"Thanks," Catherine said, taking the cup and lacing her fingers together around it.

"Could we talk?" Betsy asked, her voice candid.

Catherine had known the gesture was not of the freestanding variety. With Betsy, they never were. "Sure," she said, waving a hand at the chair beside her.

Betsy sat down, took a sip of her tea, then sighed. "How are things with you and Jeb?"

Catherine looked up in surprise. "Fine. Why do you ask?"

"May I be honest?"

"By all means," Catherine said, since to her knowledge, Betsy had never once refrained from speaking her mind, even when the other party did not want her opinion.

"I don't remember ever seeing Jeb so unhappy."

Catherine sat for a moment, too numb to respond. "Did he say something to you?" she finally said, her voice cracking a little.

Betsy took another sip of her tea, and then said, "He didn't have to."

"Oh. You can just see this in him?" Catherine asked, trying to keep her voice level.

Pity clouded Betsy's eyes. "And you can't?"

"Whatever problems Jeb and I have," she said, anger fanning through her, "I'm sure we'll work through them."

"I know things haven't been the same for any of you since Laney—"

"No, they haven't," Catherine interrupted. "But that's hardly surprising, is it?"

"Of course not," Betsy said quickly. "These things take their toll on everyone."

"These things?" Catherine bit out. "My son lost his wife—" She broke off there, her voice cracking in half.

Betsy reached over and covered her hand with her own. "I know, Catherine. I'm not trying to belittle the enormity of it. I'm just saying maybe a worse tragedy would be for this terrible thing to ruin more lives than it already has. From what I've seen, Caleb has let it get the best of him."

Fury tunneled up through Catherine's chest. She pulled her hand away and pressed her lips together, glancing across the yard where Betsy's son, Harris, stood with his arm around his very pregnant wife. Third grandchild on the way. "From your point of view, it must be so easy to judge. How could you possibly understand what Caleb has lost?"

"But there, Catherine," Betsy said softly. "You just said it. What Caleb has lost. It's his loss. But it's destroying your marriage."

She got up from the chair then, and walked back across the yard, leaving Catherine sitting at the edge of the gathering, alone.

GRACE BARELY SLEPT Friday night. She came into Sophie's room three times to ask if it was time to get up yet. The last question was asked at 4:00 a.m., and Sophie finally folded back the covers and let the child climb in beside her.

They both went back to sleep then, waking with the sunlight. Grace popped up and immediately began bouncing on the mattress. "Today's my birthday, Mama!"

"It certainly is," Sophie said, smiling.

"How many hours till the party?"

Sophie propped up on one elbow to look at the alarm clock. "Five."

Grace held up a hand, five fingers splayed. "This many?"

"That many."

They got out of bed, Grace too excited to stay still another minute. They had breakfast in their pajamas, after which Grace stood on a stool at the kitchen island and helped Sophie put icing on the sugar cookies they had baked the night before. They used green, yellow and blue, and Grace made sure each cookie had plenty. The icing was the best part, she said.

Once the cookies were done, they made punch with lime sherbet and ginger ale, then put it in the refrigerator to stay cold. After giving Grace a bath, Sophie took a quick shower and dried her hair.

The doorbell rang at ten-thirty. She looked out the window and spotted Darcy Clemen's minivan in the driveway. The two of them had started at the university around the same time as assistant professors. They'd become fast friends, a connection between them that defied Sophie's normal tendency to keep people at a distance.

Darcy and her two daughters, seven-year-old Marina and five-year-old Lauren, stood at the front door.

Sophie opened the upstairs window and called, "Come in. The door's open. I'll be right there."

Grace bounded out of the bedroom and down the stairs to meet them.

"Take your time," Darcy yelled back. "I'll corral the girls in the kitchen."

Five minutes later, she found the foursome in the kitchen admiring the birthday cake.

Darcy looked up and smiled. "Wow. It's spectacular."

"Thanks," Sophie said, proud of it. Shaped like a barn, the cake even had Dutch doors and miniature horses sticking their heads out.

"Where'd you learn to do that?"

"I actually took a cake-decorating class the summer after my divorce. I made a lot of cakes."

"I'm impressed."

Sophie gave Marina and Lauren a hug, chastised them for yet another growth spurt. "You girls are going to be taller than your mama pretty soon."

They both smiled.

On the street in front of the house, a truck slowed to a stop. Grace ran to the living-room window. "Mama, they're here!" she called back. "The donkeys are here!"

The truck and trailer were bright red and yellow, Ben's Barnyard Adventures painted on the sides. A weathered-looking older man got out. He wore a big cowboy hat, which he tipped in their direction. "Morning," he said. "One of you Dr. Owens?"

Sophie stepped forward to shake his hand. "I'm Sophie Owens."

"Ben Crawford."

"Thank you for coming. This is my daughter, Grace, and our friends Darcy, Marina and Lauren."

"Morning, ladies," he said.

"Are the donkeys in there?" Grace asked, pointing at the trailer.

"Sure are," Mr. Crawford said, smiling. "Munchin' on hay."

"Can they get out now?"

"I don't see why not." He looked at Sophie. "Where do you want us, ma'am?"

"Everything is set up in the backyard. "

He got in the truck and pulled around to the back of the house. They followed, Grace squeezing Sophie's hand tight, her blue eyes wide with excitement.

A few minutes later, Mr. Crawford lowered the tailgate and led the two miniature donkeys out.

"This is Oscar in the red halter, Lulu in the blue," he said.

Grace reached out and rubbed Lulu's neck. "She's so soft."

The little donkey nuzzled Grace's hand. She squealed with delight.

"Here," Mr. Crawford said, reaching in his pocket and pulling out a couple of sugar cubes. "You can give them one of these." He showed Grace how to hold her hand out flat with the sugar in the palm so they wouldn't accidentally nibble her fingers.

Grace was in love. Mr. Crawford hooked the donkey's lead ropes to the shaded side of the trailer and asked if she would like to brush them. Grace nodded, and he put a soft brush in her hand, showing her how to stroke in the direction the hair grew.

"I don't think you could have gotten her a better present," Darcy said.

"She loves animals," Sophie said, telling Darcy about the yellow Lab at Tucker Farm Supply.

"You lugged all that hay out here? You should have called. I could have helped."

"Actually, the man who owns the store brought it out. Caleb Tucker."

Darcy looked surprised. "Is he the dark-haired guy I've seen in there? Tall? Good-looking?"

Sophie lifted a shoulder, reaching for nonchalance. "Probably."

Darcy eyed Sophie intently. "Is that a blush in your cheeks?"

"Don't even go there," Sophie admonished.

Darcy laughed. "I think you already have."

Sophie headed for the kitchen. Darcy followed. "Not so fast," she said.

"What?" Sophie pulled Saran wrap from platters of peanut butter and jelly sandwiches carved in various shapes with the aid of cookie cutters.

"I saw that look in your eyes."

"What look?" Sophie said with a laugh.

"That I-think-he's-hot look."

"Even if I did, I assure you he barely noticed me."

"Sophie, you're way too hard on yourself."

"Realistic," she corrected with a tip of her head. "Plain Jane and Charlottesville's answer to Kevin Costner. I don't think so."

"Sometimes I wonder who you see when you look in the mirror."

Sophie managed to avoid an answer, heading outside to set the food on the picnic table beneath the tall oak at the corner of the yard. As she struggled to reposition a couple bales of hay, Sophie couldn't help wondering how Caleb Tucker had managed to carry two of them at a time.

Cars began pulling into the driveway, and the backyard was soon abuzz with three- and four-year-olds, all equally awed by Grace's birthday donkeys. Mr. Crawford had the ease of manner to get everyone lined up for a turn around the yard.

The back door opened. Sophie glanced up. Aunt Ruby and Uncle Roy walked over, Ruby with her usual take-charge manner and Roy looking unsure of his welcome. Taller than her husband by several inches, Ruby had always been the clear leader between the two, Roy the kind of man who preferred peace to conflict and usually did whatever it took to achieve it.

"Hello," Sophie said, shooting a protective glance toward Grace.

"Sophie," Aunt Ruby said, nodding once, her lined face stern, her gray hair pulled back in the same severe bun she'd worn since Sophie was a child.

Sophie hugged them both, Ruby's posture stiff and unyielding. Roy hugged her back though and gave her an awkward pat on the shoulder. She was shocked by how much older they both looked, Roy's once-black hair now nearly white.

"You look good, Sophie," he said.

"Thanks, Uncle Roy."

Darcy stepped forward just then and said, "You must be Sophie's aunt and uncle. I'm Darcy Clemens. Nice to meet you."

"Who knew Sophie had so many friends?" Ruby said to Roy as if Sophie and Darcy weren't standing there.

Darcy's eyes widened. She started to say something, but Sophie shook her head. Darcy pressed her lips together.

"Could I get you something to drink?" Sophie asked.

"Just point us in the right direction. We can help ourselves. And where's that little Grace?"

"She's on the white donkey," Sophie said, folding her arms across her chest and forcing politeness into her response.

"My goodness. Pretty little thing, isn't she? She doesn't look a bit like you."

Ruby marched toward the food table then, Roy following with downcast eyes.

As soon as they were out of earshot, Darcy blew out a snort of disbelief. "Oh, my gosh. You grew up with that?"

Sophie shrugged. "You learn to ignore her."

"Sophie. No one should have to put up with that. Why do you let her come at all?"

She was quiet for a moment, and then said, "They're the only family I have."

"Some family."

Sophie glanced down, rubbed a thumb across the back of her hand.

Darcy squeezed her arm. "I'm sorry. That sounded awful."

"It's okay, Darc. I know how it looks. Maybe I should have cut the ties long ago, but she was my mother's sister. They were nothing alike, but she's the last link I have."

"It's a shame we don't get to pick our relatives," Darcy said.

"I have no intention of letting her ruin this party. So if you don't mind, I'd rather not talk about her."

"Sure," Darcy said, sympathy in her voice.

"I'd better check on the sandwich trays," Sophie said and headed for the kitchen.

CHAPTER FOUR

WHEN SOPHIE CAME BACK out a few minutes later, Mr. Crawford had put the two donkeys in the shade with a little hay to nibble on. All the children gathered around the picnic table for cake and ice cream. Most of them ended up wearing as much on their clothes as they managed to eat, eating with the kind of unrestrained pleasure children show for simple things.

On the invitation, Sophie had asked that the guests not bring presents but items to donate to the local animal shelter in Grace's name instead. The box by the picnic table was full with paper towels, canned food, detergent, everyday items the shelter needed to stay in operation.

The children played games for forty-five minutes or so, Red Rover, Simon Says and jump rope. They all took one last ride on Oscar and Lulu, and then it was time for Mr. Crawford to load the donkeys up and take them home.

Once he'd gone, some of the children began to

leave. Those whose mothers hadn't yet come to pick them up remained, and a new game of Red Rover began.

From across the yard, Sophie watched Ruby single Grace out and kneel down beside her, one hand pushing Grace's blond hair back from her face where it had escaped her ponytail. Some protective instinct surged inside her, and it was all she could do not to storm over and sweep her daughter up in her arms.

A couple of minutes later, Ruby walked over and said it was time for them to go. "You've made a nice home for yourself, Sophie. You and Grace. I hope you're happy."

"We are," Sophie said, hearing the defensiveness in her own voice.

Ruby reached inside her oversize purse and pulled out what looked like some kind of legal document. "Oh, and by the way, there's a little something I need for you to sign."

"What is it?" Sophie asked, surprised.

"The land my daddy left to me and your mama. Roy and I have decided we'd like to build a house on it. We think ten thousand dollars is a fair price to buy you out. And since it's not something you're ever going to use—"

"What land?" Sophie asked, shaking her head.

"It's just a few acres outside of town. We never

even saw fit to tell you about it, since it wasn't worth anything."

"Ten thousand dollars sounds like something."

"We just want to make sure we're being fair to you."

Sophie glanced at Roy, who stood behind Ruby, hands in his pockets, his gaze set on the children still playing. She pressed her lips together and then said quietly, "This is something that belonged to my mother, and you never told me about it?"

"Oh, Sophie," Ruby said, her voice rising, "don't go and romanticize something that isn't a big deal. Your mother wouldn't have given two licks about that land."

"How do you know?" Sophie said, gripping the papers between clenched fists. "I have a feeling you have no idea what my mother cared about."

Ruby took a step back, as if Sophie had slapped her. "You were always such an ungrateful—"

"Ruby," Roy said. "Let's go."

Ruby stared at Sophie, her gaze hardening. "Look over the papers, Sophie. Roy and I both would appreciate your cooperation."

With that, she turned and walked away, her shoulders stiff.

Sophie glanced at the document, threw it on the chair behind her, then started clearing the picnic table of sticky plates and cups, tossing them into a big garbage bag.

Darcy came over and began helping. "They're gone, huh?"

"Yeah," Sophie said. "At least I know why they came now."

"Anything you want to talk about?"

"No."

"Okay, then. It was a wonderful party," Darcy said. "Grace had a blast."

Sophie nodded. "I think everyone had fun."

Darcy dropped a cup into the bag. "You're a wonderful mother, Sophie. Grace is a lucky little girl to have you as her family."

"No," Sophie said, a sudden catch in her throat. "I'm the one who's lucky to have her."

SOPHIE WALKED THE LAST child to the front door. Grace stood beside them, her eyes so heavy she could barely keep them open.

Darcy led her two equally tired daughters to the minivan, waving goodbye as she got into the driver's seat. Sophie picked up Grace, who immediately tucked her face into Sophie's neck and closed her eyes.

"Thank you, Mama," she said, her voice barely audible. "For the party."

"You're so very welcome, baby," Sophie said. "Are you ready for a nap?"

Grace nodded, too worn out to offer up her usual protest against sleep.

Sophie turned to close the door. A truck pulled away from the curb across the street. She glanced over her shoulder, spotting the back end of a familiar white Ford diesel pickup.

Was that Caleb Tucker's truck?

She stretched her neck but couldn't get a glimpse of the driver.

But then what would he be doing parked across from her house?

She recalled Darcy's teasing and could not deny the flutter in her stomach at the possibility of his having thought of her since yesterday.

Grace stirred in her arms. Sophie shook her head at her own foolishness, stepped inside the house and closed the door.

CALEB SHOVED THE 350's gearshift into Fourth and barreled down Ivy Run Road without regard for the residential speed limit, leaving Sophie Owens's house behind as fast as he could. He shot onto the 29 Bypass and kept the accelerator to the floor until the city began to fade behind him. Farmland appeared on either side of the truck, alfalfa fields, cornfields. He let up on the gas then, pulling air into his lungs.

On the seat beside him lay a dozen white roses wrapped in green florist paper. The breeze from his lowered window caught a petal and tossed it to the floor.

He kept driving, not letting himself think about where he was headed.

Five or so miles later, the turnoff rose up on the right. Caleb's stomach dropped. Sweat beads broke out on his forehead, and he gripped the wheel as if to let go would send him flying off to someplace he could not return from.

The cemetery was at the end of the quarter-mile gravel road. A heavy chain with a padlock blocked the entrance.

Caleb had never been given a key, and so he stopped the truck just short of the gate and turned off the engine. He sat there for a few minutes, trying to gather the courage to get out. A crow sat on one of the fence posts, its *caw-caw* the only sound in this solitary place.

The plot belonged to Laney's family. Generations of Scotts were buried here with headstones that ranged from rocks with initials scratched in as a reminder of who lay beneath to the ornate dedication that Laney's parents had insisted she have. Even through the haze that had been his reality three years ago, Caleb had thought she would much rather have been remembered with a simple rock pulled from the nearby field. But then Laney's mother had her own way of doing things, and all decisions in the Scott family were made her way.

Caleb reached across the seat for the roses and got out of the truck. His palms were damp and left marks on the florist paper.

He stepped over the heavy chain and walked the short distance to the graveyard. A black wrought-iron gate lay at the end of a stone footpath. Caleb lifted the handle. It made a rusty rasp of protest.

Laney's headstone was in the far right-hand corner of the neatly mowed enclosure. He weaved his way through the other graves, most of the head-stones indicating average to long life spans, another arrow of unfairness that Laney should be here with only thirty-one years spent on this earth.

He stopped just short of her grave.

Others had been here today; the grass in front of the headstone was covered with four different arrangements of flowers.

Something inside him had locked up, and he couldn't remember how to make his arms or legs move. His heart thudded heavily, and the metallic taste of panic stung the back of his throat.

Finally, he bent down on one knee and placed

his own offering to the side of the others, recognizing the enormous spray of carnations as favorites of Mary's. Laney had hated carnations.

The wind threw out a short gust, scattering a few of the rose petals across the grave. It seemed a better idea to him, so Caleb began pulling the white petals from the stems, letting them fall where they would.

When the stems were bare, he sat down on the grass, weakened as if he'd just finished a miles-long run.

"Wonders never cease."

Startled, Caleb jerked around, ran a hand across the back of his neck. "I didn't hear you pull up, Mary," he said.

"I'm sure if you had, you would have left," she said, walking over to stop just short of the headstone. She wore black, head to toe. Her once-blond hair was now gray. Grief had etched hard lines into her face, and she was so thin, her clothes hung on her.

"I thought you'd already been here today," Caleb said.

"I had. With Emmitt. I wanted to come back by myself."

Silence weighed heavy between them. Caleb got to his feet. "So, how're you doing, Mary?"

She shrugged, tipping her head. "Some days are better than others. And you?"

"Pretty much just like that."

"I keep expecting to hear you've moved on. Found someone else."

"Expecting or hoping?"

"Why should it matter to me one way or the other?"

"Why should it?" he threw back.

Mary folded her arms across her chest and stared at her daughter's headstone. "I know you loved her, Caleb, but—"

"But what, Mary?" he interrupted, his voice hard. "But if she hadn't married me, none of this would have happened? Is that what you were going to say?"

Mary stared out past the cemetery at some point in the distance, not answering for a long while. When she finally did, she said, "Laney deserved more than you had to give her."

The words cut deep. "I know you lost your daughter, Mary," Caleb said. "But I lost my wife, too. And I *did* love her."

She looked directly at him then, her eyes filled with a piercing grief. "Sometimes, that's just not enough though, is it?" she said. She turned then and walked away. He watched as she got in her car, backed up and drove off.

He stood there for a long time, then finally dropped onto his knees next to the grave.

He had not come here once since the funeral.

Before today, just the thought of doing so had filled him with instant resistance. He couldn't bear to return to the place where he had left her, this spot out in the country that had marked the end of their life together. Nor could he bear to think of his young, beautiful wife here in this lonely place.

Now that he was here, he saw the senselessness in his thinking. This spot was no more than a memorial to her physical presence on earth. Laney was wherever the good went. This he knew in the marrow of his bones.

But her child was here. In the same town where he worked and lived.

He'd somehow imagined she would have been adopted by someone out of the area. It hadn't been a stipulation, so he could hardly blame the agency.

A soft swoosh of wind lifted the boughs of a nearby pine tree. He felt the touch on his shoulder, soothing, comforting. He looked around. There was no one there, and yet he felt the presence of his wife as surely as if he were looking at her.

He wondered again if he was losing his mind, if this was how it happened. Truth and desperate hope merging to form new reality.

Whatever the explanation, the pain inside him softened and dissolved into something more neutral. Something bearable so that his mind cleared like fog dissipating before a waiting sun.

He had driven out to Sophie Owens's house today to convince himself he had been wrong. That the resemblance between the little girl and his wife was nothing more than his imagination looking for some new way to reach Laney when she was no longer reachable.

He'd spent the night on the porch in the old rocker, unable to face the bed they had shared, and he had never had the heart to replace. He hadn't slept, but sat up wide awake until the sun rose, the knowledge burning in him that he had seen with his own eyes the child to whom Laney had given birth.

After three years of blocking his mind to her existence, she had appeared right in front of him, as if that, too, had been part of some plan laid out for him without his consent.

The child's face hung in his mind now like a newly taken snapshot, and in her likeness to his wife, he imagined the children they had hoped to have together and wondered if they would have looked like Laney, too.

BECAUSE CATHERINE WAS miserable, they left North Carolina a day early and drove all the way back with no more than ten words spoken between them. It had been that way all weekend, and regardless of how many times Jeb asked her, Catherine would not tell him what was wrong. She had put up yet another wall between them, and he was beginning to feel the hopelessness of ever getting through again.

They got home around five, each of them unpacking their suitcases in silence. Catherine was downstairs in the kitchen starting supper when he walked through on his way outside to get the newspaper.

She stood by the sink, slicing apples, halving each one and then scooping out the center with a quickness that made her agitation clear.

He stopped at the door, walked across the floor and put his hand on her shoulder. He felt her stiffen beneath his touch, but forced himself not to let go.

"Don't I have a right to know what happened, Cath? At least then, I might be able to defend myself."

She continued slicing, then stopped and said, "You should have asked Betsy."

He restrained a sigh. His big sister could rarely resist meddling. "What did she say?"

Catherine turned, her blue eyes meeting his. "Basically that I need to wake up and realize how miserable you are."

He opened his mouth to deny it, then stood there mute when the words wouldn't come out.

Her eyes widened. She turned back to the sink, one hand gripping the edge.

"Betsy shouldn't have interfered," he said, keeping his voice soft. "But how long are we going to go on like this, Cath?"

She dropped her chin, her shoulders suddenly shaking with silent weeping.

An actual pain stabbed through Jeb's heart. "Baby, come here," he said, turning her to face him. He put his arms around her and rubbed the back of her hair with his hand. "Shh. Don't cry."

"It's like there's this black cloud over me," she said after a minute or two, "and I can't see through it anymore. Most days, I don't want to try."

"Maybe you need to see somebody," he said carefully. "There's medicine for this kind of thing—"

She stiffened again, pulling back with a look of pure fear. "I'm not sick, Jeb."

He ran a hand through his hair. "That's not what I meant."

"What did you mean?" she asked, her voice sharp.

Jeb stared at her, thinking about Elaine, Catherine's mother, and the things Catherine had seen growing up. Doctor after doctor. Medications that had helped until Elaine had stopped taking them, any progress she had made eroding beneath a fresh wave of depression. Her eventual institutionalization. Catherine had talked to him about it in bits and pieces early on in their marriage, but at some point, she'd just seemed to close the door and not let herself revisit any of it.

"Catherine," he said.

She turned away, reached for a pot from the stove and placed the apples in it. "Can we not talk about this now?"

"I'm afraid if we don't it's going to swallow us both."

She went still for a moment, then filled the pot with water, set it back on the stove. "Everything's going to be fine. You'll see."

But it wasn't fine. And he knew with the worst kind of sinking feeling that all the things wrong between them weren't going to fix themselves. He would walk to the moon and back for this woman he'd married thirty-seven years ago.

But the truth, he knew in his gut. She wasn't going to let him.

CHAPTER FIVE

AFTER CHURCH ON SUNDAY, Sophie and Grace turned in at the wooden sign marking the entrance to the Open Hearts Animal Home off route 29. The back of the Volvo was weighed down with donated items.

Open Hearts had bought an old farm out in the country for its facility, converting the house and barn as well as a couple of other buildings into housing for unwanted dogs and cats. Sophie stopped the car in front of the house where a sign read Visitors Enter Here, Please. She got Grace out of the car seat, and they went inside to the registration desk.

A woman appeared from the hallway to their left. Tall and thin with crinkly blue eyes, she wore faded denim overalls. Her dark hair hung in a braid to the center of her back. "Hello," she said. "I'm Teresa Moore, the shelter director. Could I help you?"

"I'm Sophie Owens. We spoke on the phone last week. My daughter, Grace, has some things to donate from her birthday party."

"Oh, yes. How wonderful of you, Grace."

Grace dropped her eyes at the woman's compliment, obviously pleased.

They unloaded the car, bringing everything into the foyer and stacking it in the corner. It was an impressive amount of stuff.

"I can't tell you how much all of this will be appreciated," Teresa said, shaking her head.

"You're welcome," Sophie replied. "Would it be possible for Grace to pick out a dog for her birthday?"

Grace looked up at Sophie, her little mouth making a small O of surprise, her eyes widening. "Really, Mama?"

"Really," Sophie said, running a hand across her daughter's silky hair.

"Just follow me," Teresa said, waving them down the hall. At the end, she opened a door, and they were greeted by a chorus of excited barks.

"Everyone in here is available for adoption. They've all had shots and been spayed or neutered if they're old enough."

Grace stood for a moment, clearly not sure where to look first.

"Come on, sweetie," Sophie said, taking her hand. They walked down the aisle, greeted at each cage with boisterous tail wagging. There was one exception. A medium-size black-and-white dog, notable in that she was the only one who had stayed at the back of her cage, her head resting on stretched-out paws, looking as if she'd long ago given up hope of a different life. Grace stopped at the dog's door. "What's her name?"

"Lily," Teresa said.

Across the aisle, a chorus of excited yipping drew Grace's attention. Five round-bellied puppies were conducting a wrestling match in the middle of the run. "Oh!" Grace bolted over and squatted down to peer through the chain-link door.

Teresa smiled. "Aren't they cute? They're eight weeks old as of yesterday, so they can be adopted now, too."

"Oh, Mama," Grace breathed.

"They're adorable," Sophie said.

"Would you like to play with them?" Teresa asked.

Grace nodded. Teresa opened the door, and they all bounded out into the aisle, tumbling over one another. Grace giggled and ran after them. They played for several minutes while Sophie and Teresa watched with smiles on their faces.

"Do you want to take one of the puppies, Grace?" Sophie asked.

Grace looked up from the concrete floor where she sat with three of them climbing up her lap. She looked at the puppies and then at the older dog who had yet to get up from her position at the back of the cage.

"Why does Lily look so sad?"

"Lily has been here a long time," Teresa said.

"Is she sad because nobody's picked her?"

Teresa lifted one shoulder and sighed. "No matter how well we take care of them, it's not the same as having a home."

Grace glanced down at the wiggling puppies on her lap, then back to Lily who was gazing at her with eyes devoid of any expectation. Grace remained silent for several moments. And then said, "Mama, can I see Lily?"

"Is it all right, Teresa?"

"Of course." She put the puppies back in their cage where they continued their wrestling. She opened Lily's door and looked at Grace. "You can go in and pet her. She's really good with children."

Grace walked to the back of the run, squatted and rubbed Lily's long coat. "She's soft."

"I suspect she has some cocker spaniel in her. And some type of setter, judging from her coat. She's a very sweet dog. Probably the most unde-manding one here."

Lily's tailed thumped once. Grace kept rubbing her. After a few moments, Lily stood up, her head low, tail tucked.

Grace glanced back at the puppies, then looked at Sophie. "I want to pick Lily, Mama."

Lily raised her head and licked Grace's cheek.

"Lily, it is," Sophie said. "Let's take her home."

LILY NEEDED A COLLAR and leash, a doggy bed and a bone to chew on.

So proclaimed Grace, along with her desire to buy them at the place where Noah lived.

"I want to tell him about Lily, Mama."

There were other places they could have gone Lily-shopping, other places that were closer than Tucker's. But Sophie reasoned that Grace liked the yellow Lab, and why shouldn't they give the store their business when its owner had been nice enough to haul that hay out to their house for them?

After Sophie got back from her morning classes on Monday, she changed clothes, brushed some fresh powder across her nose, put on a medium-pink lipstick she usually only wore at night.

Halfway down the hall, she turned back to the bathroom, pulled out the rubber band that had anchored her hair at her neck, brushed through it a few times, started to put it back up, then at the last second, left it loose around her shoulders.

CALEB SPENT MOST OF the day at the store, working in the office upstairs and watching the register out front while Macy went to lunch.

It was almost one-thirty when the front door dinged. Sophie and Grace Owens came in and stood on the other side of the counter. A hot and cold blast of emotion washed over him.

"Afternoon, Dr. Owens," he said, aiming his voice toward steady and even when everything else inside him rocked like a dingy on storm-churned seas.

"Hello," she said.

"Hay bales hold up?"

"Yes. They did." She cleared her throat, a small, feminine sound that somehow stood out in contrast with her precise, no-nonsense manner. "Thank you again for bringing them out. And, please, it's Sophie."

Caleb nodded, aware of the stiffness in his face, seeing its effect on the woman, who glanced down and put a hand on the little girl's shoulder.

"We need a bed and a collar for my new dog," the child said.

Caleb had no choice but to look at her then, and it was like having someone stick a knife in the center of his heart. Laney's eyes. She had Laney's eyes. "A new dog?"

"Her name's Lily. She gets to sleep with me."

Noah trotted over from his post by Russell's perch, a stuffed toy in his mouth, wagging his tail and making a happy circle around the little girl.

"Hi, Noah," she said and giggled when he nudged her leg with the toy.

"Easy, Noah," Caleb said.

Noah sat and looked at her with adoring eyes, his tail swishing back and forth on the wood floor like a windshield wiper.

"We'll just look around if that's all right," Sophie said.

He was having a hard time thinking of her as *Sophie,* even though she'd introduced herself that way. *Sophie* was personal. He didn't want personal. He wanted distance. He wanted to rewind the tape and go back to Thursday morning when she and that little girl had walked into the store. He wanted to redo things so that he stayed upstairs instead of coming down to help her. Then none of this would ever have happened.

"Sure," he said, not meeting her eyes. "Let me know if I can help with anything."

Noah followed them around the store, trailing after the little girl aisle to aisle, love struck. Caleb watched from up front, more discreet than Noah, but equally unable to take his eyes off her. Like Laney, there was something about her that drew people, a warm glow that made her seem almost lit from within.

Sophie came back to the register. "I was wondering if you could recommend a good dog food," she said. "I've never bought any, so I really have no idea—"

Caleb moved around the counter, accidentally brushing arms with her. She stepped to the side quickly, bumping into a water-hose cart. On impulse, he reached out to steady her.

"I'm sorry," she said, looking embarrassed.

Caleb pulled his hand back as if it had just encountered a red-hot surface, then nodded and headed to where he kept the dog food. "We've got several brands. I can show you the one I feed Noah. It's a little pricey, but it's certified human-grade food with omega-3 and six EFAs. Good for their coat, and it has some extra antioxidants, as well."

She followed, arms crossed at her waist. "That sounds good."

Caleb pulled a bag from the shelf and held it out for her inspection. "How much does she weigh?"

"Forty-five pounds or so?"

"This would do then."

"Okay," she said. "We'll take that one."

"Anything else?"

"Food and water bowls."

"Over here," he said, moving a few steps up the aisle. "Stainless steel or plastic?"

"Stainless steel."

He picked up two. "These all right?"

She nodded, keeping her gaze on the bowls. She hadn't looked at him directly since they'd left the front counter. She bent slightly forward and her hair swung free of its anchor behind her ear. She reached up, tucked it back, still without looking at him. In that unobserved moment, he noted a few details about her. Still no rings on her hands. A watch with a plain leather band circled her left wrist. Crisp white blouse and equally wrinkle-free khaki pants. Dark brown loafers. Career woman in weekend casual.

Since he was sixteen years old, there had been one woman to whom he compared all others. And he did so now with the complete acceptance that she would be his only benchmark for the rest of his life.

Individually, Laney's features had been extraordinary. Wide blue eyes with thick, fringed lashes. Straight, small nose. Lips and cheeks that had never needed cosmetics for color. Caleb had long been used to people staring at his wife in admiration, even though she herself had never seen it, always pointing out what she considered her shortcomings.

Sophie Owens did not strike him as the kind of

woman people often stared at. Her features were closer to ordinary than extraordinary. Brown eyes, medium blond hair, high cheekbones. But the overall effect was attractive in an understated sort of way. And he wondered what her life was like, why she had chosen to adopt a child and what it was that had brought their paths to this intersection.

He gathered up the bowls and the bag of food, carrying them to the front where she had left the things they'd already picked out. The silence between them uncomfortable, Caleb cleared his throat once before punching each of the items into a computer that balked regularly under any touch other than Macy's. Today was no exception. It refused to print a receipt. Caleb finally gave up and looked at Sophie.

"All right if I send you a printout of your purchase in the mail? I can't seem to find the right button."

"Sure," she said. "That'll be fine."

He wrote down her address, and then carried her stuff out to the car while she went to get Grace. They met him outside, the child talking nonstop about Noah and how maybe Lily would like to have a cat to play with, too.

Sophie unlocked the car. Caleb opened the back and put everything inside. He closed the lid and stepped up on the sidewalk. A moment of stark awkwardness fell over them. How many times could he do this? How long could he look at that little girl and keep his face clear of the agony inside him?

"Well, thank you again," she said, buckling Grace into her car seat and opening her own door.

"You're welcome," he said, then turned and went inside.

DRIVING HOME, SOPHIE GLANCED in the rearview mirror. Grace was fast asleep, clutching Lily's new toy in one hand. Sophie turned off the radio, wanting the quiet.

What was she to make of that look on Caleb Tucker's face just before he'd abruptly gone back in the store?

She had put Grace in her car seat, and when she'd turned to take the bags and thank him, he'd been staring at her daughter. It was as if a shadow had come over him, and through the narrow crack in his composure, she had glimpsed something that looked like the most intense pain she'd ever seen on another person's face.

Had he lost a child of his own?

She knew next to nothing about him, but Sophie liked to put labels on things. Sum them up so she knew exactly what she was dealing with. Good or bad, she wanted to know, because only in knowing could a person choose the safe direction.

Back there, in that moment, it had felt as if there was something she should know.

Okay, so maybe she was reaching, overreacting. Maybe it was nothing more than that he was in a hurry, and she'd taken up enough of his time.

Ahead of her, a car slowed for two cyclists riding with traffic. She tapped the brake, straddled the centerline until she'd gone around them. She recognized them as two professors from the university. She raised a hand in greeting and drove on.

Most of the men in Sophie's circle were nothing like Caleb Tucker. They wore tweed blazers and khaki pants, glasses that stayed perched on the ends of their noses. Drove Subarus and played chess on Thursday nights.

Caleb Tucker wore Wrangler jeans and boots. Soft cotton shirts that looked as though they'd never held the starch of a dry cleaner. She had no idea what he did on Thursday nights. And she doubted that he cycled on weekends in tight stretch pants.

But he looked at her with questions in his eyes.

How did she explain the almost magnetic pull to drive out there today?

She had no answers, and so, no way of identifying the safe direction where he was concerned.

But something told her she should keep her

distance. A small but persistent voice that said it would be dangerous to do otherwise.

Sophie's mother had once told her that voice was God's megaphone, and even though she'd been seven years old at the time, she had never forgotten.

She glanced at Grace again in the mirror now, her small face almost angelic in sleep.

And she had her answer.

They wouldn't be going back out to Tucker's.

CHAPTER SIX

AFTER MACY GOT BACK from lunch, Caleb drove home, too restless to stay at the store. He needed space around him. He let Noah in the house, went to the barn and grabbed a halter, called the three horses grazing in the nearby pasture. They loped to the gate. He put the halter on Winnie and led her to the barn.

She was Laney's mare, and Laney had been the last one on her. She'd always been a handful, too much horse for the weekend ride his wife had bought her to be. But she'd ridden the mare every Saturday and Sunday, taking off through the fields at a full gallop, her hair and the mare's tail flying out behind them like flags of freedom.

Caleb ran a brush over the horse, picked out her hoofs, threw on a pad and saddle, then climbed up. He could feel the mare's energy beneath his seat, like a spring ready to pop. They jigged out of the barn, down the lane between the house and pasture, and he let her go. Her hooves pounded the old dirt road. They followed it a quarter mile or so,

then cut through a hay field he'd just mowed last
week. He wished they could ride straight for the
horizon and over the edge into whatever peace
was to be found there.

Because there was no peace for him here.

Midway out the field, he slowed the horse to a
lope, then a jog and finally a walk, much to her dis-
pleasure. He was convinced she would run until
she dropped. She had that kind of heart, and that
was what had drawn Laney to her. She'd bought
her at a stockyard sale where the mare had ended
up after throwing some fool kid who'd been riding
her with two-inch spurs. He'd spent the morning
telling everybody there the horse had the devil in
her, better let her go with the dog-food guys. As
soon as Laney had heard that, they'd been buying
the mare outright for more cash than the boy had
ever hoped to see for her. From that point on, the
mare had belonged to Laney in every sense of the
word. Caleb sometimes thought the horse had
grieved as much as he had when she was gone.

They circled the back side of the field now,
stopping short of his parent's house, an updated
version of his own. Two-story, white frame with a
porch on the front.

His mother was working in the garden, a big
straw hat sitting low on her head. She looked up,
spade in hand, spotted him and waved. Caleb gave

the horse a soft squeeze with his legs and they headed toward her.

"Thought Dad said you were at the store," she said, getting to her feet and pushing the rim of the hat back so she could see him.

"Decided to leave a little early," he said, ducking his mother's steady gaze.

She pressed her lips together now the way she did when she knew there was more to the story, but intended to let it unravel at its own pace. She knew him, maybe better than he knew himself.

"Mind if I walk with you a while?" she asked.

"Be glad for the company," he said, admitting to himself then that this had been his destination all along. He needed to unload the weight on his chest. Thought it might break him in half if he didn't.

"Just give me a sec," she said.

Less than five minutes later, she was back with Sally-Mae, the little quarter-horse mare she'd been riding the past twenty years. She never used a saddle, preferring to ride bareback. The mare was as wide as a sofa, and basically had one gear: slow walk.

They ambled out across the field, the two horses touching noses in greeting, both emitting short, excited whinnies. Neither Caleb nor his mother said anything for a good while, but rode in quiet companionship as they had many other times.

It was the kind of day that made a person

grateful to be outdoors. The April sunshine was warm on their backs, a light breeze lifting the heat from their skin.

"I saw her," Caleb finally said, feeling his mother's gaze settle on him and yet unable to look at her for the concern he knew would have sprung to her eyes.

"Who, son?" she asked, her voice careful.

"Laney's baby."

Catherine stopped her horse and dropped the reins. "What did you say?"

Caleb still couldn't look at her, didn't think he could stand to see the fresh grief on her face. "She's three, and she looks so much like Laney, you'd swear you were seeing a ghost."

Catherine slid off the mare, stood there in stunned silence while her horse began to graze.

Caleb got off and ground tied his own horse. The mare dropped her head to the green grass, as well. He allowed himself a glance at his mother, then abruptly turned away, the pain in her eyes too much a reflection of what was in his own heart.

"Are you sure?" she asked, the question breaking in half at the end.

He nodded once.

She came to him then, put her arms around him and began to cry. They held each other for a long time, encircled by sorrow as fresh as yesterday.

"I'm sorry, Mom," Caleb finally said. "I shouldn't have put you through this all over again."

"Oh, son, I would hope you'd never consider keeping it to yourself. You've carried too much of this alone as it is."

He set his gaze on the horizon, struggled for a foothold against the anguish raging inside him. "Did I do the right thing, Mom?"

"In giving her up?"

He nodded.

"That child was as much a victim of what happened to Laney as the rest of us. How could you have accepted her then, and who could blame you? You'd just been through months and months of pure hell. She would have represented all of that, and no child should start life with that mantle hung on her. You gave her innocence, Caleb."

"I didn't do it for her, Mom," he said, shaking his head. "I did it for me. I look at her, and all I see is Laney. No one else. Just Laney."

Again, pain flashed over his mother's still beautiful face. "How did this happen?"

"She came into the store with the woman who adopted her. She's a professor at the university."

Catherine sighed, the sound coming from deep inside her, heavy, burdened. "Does she seem happy?"

"Yes. She's beautiful. And there's this…glow to her. I can't explain it. Angelic almost."

"Caleb." She hesitated, visibly searching for words. "Find your peace in this. The child is loved. Wanted. Let her go, and get on with your life. You've grieved for so long. You're a young man. There's so much more for you out there if you will just let it in. Give someone else a chance. Make another life for yourself."

They were words she'd wanted to say to him for a long time. Caleb knew this. For three years, he had remained in neutral, moving nowhere, simply existing, as if waiting for life to do a rapid-fire reverse, give him a chance to make another choice, to go with his wife the day she'd innocently driven away from the farm and never come back.

His mother put her hand on his arm, gave it a pleading squeeze. "It's time, son. Maybe that's why this happened. Maybe you needed to see that the child was all right before you could go on with your life."

"Maybe so," he said.

Why then didn't the answer fit the shape of the hole inside him?

JEB WENT TO the Whole Foods Market in Charlottesville and bought Catherine's favorite things for dinner that night. Atlantic salmon for grilling, baby spinach leaves for a salad and a bar of ridiculously expensive unsweetened German chocolate, which they both agreed made the best brownies imaginable.

He got home around four-thirty, knowing she wouldn't be back from her hair appointment until nearly six.

He removed everything from the grocery bags, then got busy mixing ingredients for the brownies, popping them into a preheated oven and setting the timer so he'd remember to take them out when they were still soft in the middle.

Next, he made a cilantro marinade for the salmon, drizzled it over the steaks and set them in the refrigerator. Pulling an oversize bowl from the kitchen cabinet, he threw in the spinach, diced an onion and a cucumber and made a dressing of olive oil and lemon juice.

With fifteen minutes to spare, he ran upstairs and took a quick shower, dressing in jeans and a light blue shirt she'd once said she liked him in.

When he heard her footsteps in the foyer, he popped the cork on a bottle of chardonnay and poured two glasses.

She walked into the kitchen, stopping in the doorway with a look of surprise on her face.

He lifted both glasses and handed her one. "Happy anniversary, Cath," he said.

She stared at him, started to say something,

then stopped. A sob broke free from her throat. "Oh, Jeb," she said. "I forgot."

He reached out to put a hand on her shoulder. "Hey," he said, "it's all right. Didn't I forget once a few years ago? So we're even."

She dropped into a kitchen chair, her face in her hands, crying in earnest now.

He knelt down in front of her. "What's wrong, Catherine? This has to be about more than forgetting our anniversary."

She shook her head, drew in a deep breath, and looked up at him. "Caleb stopped by this afternoon. He saw the child."

A heavy pause and then he said, "What child?"

"Laney's child."

Jeb sat back on his heels, disbelief thrumming through him. "How?"

"In the store. With the woman who adopted her."

He stood, raking a hand through his hair. "What did Caleb say?"

"He's confused. Questioning the decision he made to give her up."

"There was no other choice."

Catherine didn't answer right away, then said, "That's what I thought, too. But since he left here, I keep thinking, what if he hadn't given her up? In that child, he would still have a part of Laney."

Jeb stared at his wife, unable to believe what he was hearing. "It's done, Cath. Irreversible."

She bit her lip. "Is it?"

He shook his head, glanced at the table he'd set with their wedding china. "I keep thinking we're going to get past this. That one day we'll be able to put this awful thing behind us. But I've been wrong, haven't I? I've been wrong."

THAT NIGHT, CALEB SAT OUT on the porch again, the radio's poignant offering identifiable to him only as Puccini.

He fell asleep sometime around midnight. The dream was immediate, as if waiting only for him to close his eyes. His wife as beautiful as the day he'd married her, except she was crying. Her face ravaged by grief.

He tried to go to her, held out his hand, but she remained just out of reach. He called her name. She couldn't hear him. Fear welled inside him, his heart a pounding drum.

He could not get to her, could not save her now as he had been unable to save her before.

He awoke abruptly, sat straight up in the chair, pain searing his chest. A whip-poor-will called out from a nearby tree. The radio had lost its music. Static hummed in the air.

Caleb gripped the arms of the old rocker, his

knuckles white against the dark grain. And he understood then in the deepest part of himself that all this time, Laney's tears had not been for herself, but for the child he had given away.

ON THE FOLLOWING FRIDAY, Sophie worked in her campus office to catch up on grading the papers her British lit class had turned in the day before. Sophie liked to stay on top of her workload, getting essays or tests back to her students by the next class when possible. She reasoned that if she expected promptness from them, she expected it from herself as well.

A knock sounded on her closed door.

"Come in," she called out.

The door opened and Caleb Tucker stepped inside.

Sophie sat back in her chair, one hand at her chest. A dozen questions scattered through her thoughts, each too slippery to get a hold on. Two things registered. The room seemed considerably smaller than it had just moments before. And she wished she'd chosen something to wear other than the plain jeans and white T-shirt she'd pulled from the closet that morning.

She stood. "Caleb. Come in. What a surprise."

He closed the door behind him, his face set, serious. His gaze swept the office, lingering for a moment on the framed degrees on the wall behind her. B.A. Master's. Ph.D. "I wondered if I might have a few minutes of your time," he said.

Sophie's heart kicked up its pace for no reason she could explain other than that this man had crept into her thoughts repeatedly over the past few weeks. To find him standing in her office was more than a little unsettling.

"Sit down, please," she said, waving a hand at the chair in front of her desk.

"Thank you," he said. "I'm fine."

Her initial surprise at seeing him gave way to an inexplicable unease. "What can I do for you, Caleb?"

He went to the window and stared out at the manicured lawn with its neatly pruned boxwood hedges. Sophie studied the set of his shoulders, centered, it seemed, with some rigid tension she only just now noticed.

He turned and looked at her, his eyes heavy with pain. "There's no easy way for me to say this, so I'll just put it straight out. I believe my wife gave birth to the little girl you adopted."

The words came at her in slow motion, as if they'd been delivered from miles and miles away. She dropped into the chair behind her, her legs suddenly unable to support her. "What did you say?"

He pulled a photo from his pocket and handed it to her.

She stared at it, leaden fear settling in her stomach. The picture had obviously been taken years ago, but the child captured there could have been Grace. A fingerprint could not have been more telling.

"I made an awful mistake," he said, "and gave her away."

The words hung there between them. In that moment, the thing Sophie had feared most since the day she'd received the incredible gift of her daughter happened. And her world blew apart into a million tiny pieces.

CALEB PICKED UP THE coffee mug from Sophie Owens's desk, stepped into the hall and filled it with water from the fountain outside her door. He did so quickly, then covered the distance back to her chair with long strides. Her face had bleached of color, as if someone had opened a vein and drained her of life.

"Here, drink this," he said, squatting beside her chair and lifting the cup to her lips.

She sipped from it, her eyes wide and slow-blinking with the weight of shock. She swallowed once, twice, then pulled away from him as if she'd suddenly realized she was sitting next to dynamite. "Why? Why are you telling me this?"

He stood, went to the window and stared at the

students sitting on the lawn under a warm spring sun. Wished for the simplicity of life as it had seemed when he'd been their age. Nothing more to think about than hitting the books and ordering a pizza for dinner. Nothing so complicated as tearing a woman's life apart with a single piece of information.

The chair slid back. She came to the window and stood beside him. "Look at me, please," she said, her voice a hoarse whisper.

For a few drawn-out seconds, he kept his gaze firmly on the scene outside the window. He was tired of pain. Tired of his own. He didn't want to take on anyone else's. And yet he had come here today, propelled by something he did not fully understand.

He turned around and sucked in a breath at the physical slam of regret for the grief now pooled in Sophie Owens's eyes.

"I never saw the baby," he said, the words torn from him. "I couldn't let myself. And then you walked into the store with her. She looks so much like Laney."

Sophie flinched, as if the name brought with it another slap of reality.

"I gave away the last piece of her I'll ever have."

"What is it you want from me?" she asked, her voice barely audible.

"To fix the wrong I did to my wife," he said. "I want her child back."

"GET OUT," SOPHIE SAID, her voice calm and then rising, "Now! Go! Please! Get out!"

Caleb stared at her for several long moments, clear regret etched in his face. He said nothing more, but quietly did as she asked.

When he was gone, she grabbed a stapler from her desk, hurled it at the door with all her strength. It flew apart, landed on the floor in a mound of broken pieces.

She put her hand over her mouth, forcing back a scream. She stood, swayed, her chest rising and falling as if her lungs had forgotten how to process air.

Strangely, the moment was exactly as she had dreamed it in the awful nightmares she'd had the first year of Grace's life.

Nightmares in which a woman showed up at her front door, informed Sophie that Grace wasn't really hers, that there had been a mistake.

And yet it was different.

She'd never imagined it would be a man knocking at her door with those terrifying words on his lips. Always, it had been the mother who realized the horror of what she had done. The mother who came back for the child she had given away.

She felt tricked somehow, as if she'd been given the wrong description of the enemy and had been watching out for someone completely different.

Caleb Tucker had come here today to take her daughter away from her. His wife's child, he'd said. Did that mean Grace wasn't his? Had his wife had an affair?

Sophie moved to the window, watched him cross the lawn, weariness in the slight slump of his shoulders, in the heaviness of his step. She felt some measure of satisfaction that his appearance here had come with a price.

She forced herself to reach for focus, for calm. She couldn't panic. Had to remain clearheaded, figure out what to do. Her attorney. She needed to call her attorney. Irene would know how to handle this. Make everything normal again.

She glanced at the broken stapler strewn across the floor. There had to be a way to put everything back the way it had been before he'd come here today.

Hands shaking, she grabbed her Palm Pilot from the desk. She scrolled through for the number, then reached for the phone, an awful sense of déjà vu settling over her. For three years, she had lived in fear of this possibility, waiting for its arrival, as if she had known all along the inevitability of losing what had become most precious to her.

As a child, she'd once lost everyone she loved, this same choking emptiness rising inside her like high tide, threatening to wash away anything in its path.

She'd grown up in a home where she wasn't wanted. Married a man who'd ended up making her feel the same way. After divorcing Peter, she'd vowed to carve out her own happiness. Make the life for herself that she had always wanted. A child, a family.

She had that life now. A daughter she loved more than she'd ever thought it possible to love another living being.

No one was going to take her away. No one.

CHAPTER SEVEN

"DON'T PANIC, SOPHIE."

Irene Archer's voice had the soothing quality of a professional who knew her job. A partner in Charlottesville's largest law firm—Quinn, Lewis, Day—Irene had reached her rung on the ladder by maintaining confidence under the most daunting circumstances, conveying quiet conviction in her arguments to client, judge and jury alike.

"I need your voice of reason, Irene, because what I'm thinking now is to pack a suitcase, grab Grace and go somewhere where he'll never find us."

"I think that's a bit drastic at this point," Irene reasoned. "Tell me everything he said to you. And don't leave out a single detail. I need to know it all."

Sophie repeated the conversation, everything she could remember, told her, too, of how she'd met him at the hardware store, how he'd hauled the hay for Grace's party home for them, leaving out the part where she'd found him attractive, thought about him a few too many times since then.

"That's when he recognized her," she said. "Oh, dear God, I wish I'd never gone in there."

"How could you have known?" Irene had taken off her attorney's hat, her voice full of compassion. "We'll deal with this, Sophie. The important thing is for you to stay strong. The adoption was conducted to the letter of the law. You have that on your side."

"Can he challenge it?" Sophie's voice wavered.

"Anything can be challenged. Could he win? I don't think so, but life could get rough for a while. Can you handle that?"

"I would walk through fire for her, Irene."

"I know you would."

Another wave of panic washed through Sophie, weakening her legs so that she had to sit down. "Oh, God, I couldn't bear to lose her."

"You're not going to," Irene said softly. "Let's wait and see what happens. Maybe he'll have a crisis of conscience. Realize what he's about to do. Change his mind."

Sophie shook her head. "I don't think so. There's something in his eyes, Irene…grief like I've never seen."

"Sophie." There was steel in her voice now. "It's important that you keep your distance from that kind of assessment. You're going to need every ounce of impartiality you can summon. You can't afford sympathy. Caleb Tucker is a threat to you. Don't forget it, okay?"

Sophie sighed, dropped her head onto the palm of her hand. "Okay," she said.

"If he's serious about this, you'll be getting a call from his attorney. Let's just wait and see what happens. You've played by the rules, and the rules are on your side."

It was true. From any standpoint of logic, Sophie knew it.

Why then did the words feel like a threadbare sweater in a winter wind, bringing absolutely no comfort at all?

FROM SOPHIE OWENS'S office, Caleb drove straight to his parents' house. He found his dad out back working on the lawn mower. "Mom here?" he asked.

"She's inside making some soup."

"Could you come in for a minute, Dad?"

Jeb put down the rag in his hand and followed Caleb into the house.

Catherine turned from the stove when they walked in the kitchen, wiping her hands on her apron. "Caleb," she said. "I didn't hear you pull up."

"Maybe you two better sit down."

Catherine's face lost its color. "What is it, son?"

"Please," Caleb said.

Catherine sat. Jeb took the chair across the table from her. Caleb stood behind one of the ladder-backs, his hands gripping the top rung, his knuckles white.

"I went to see the woman who adopted Laney's baby today," he said. "I've spoken to a lawyer who's willing to help me try to get her back."

Both his parents sat as still as stone for several moments. Finally, Catherine slid back her chair, sudden tears streaming down her face. "Excuse me," she said and left the room.

Jeb's concerned gaze followed her, then returned to Caleb, his eyes weighted with sadness. "Don't do this, son," he said, his voice low. "You made a decision for what seemed best for that child, and not a person in this world could blame you for it."

"I blame myself."

"That's just it," he said. "You blame yourself for what happened to Laney. I learned a long time ago that we can't go around thinking we have a whole lot to do with what goes on in this world. Sometimes bad things just happen. To good people who've never done a thing to deserve it. Some people get to be movie stars, and some people work in coal mines their whole lives. I have to believe it all gets evened out in the end."

Caleb looked away and said, "I gave that baby away because I couldn't stand to look at her. I did that for me, not because I was thinking of what was best for her."

"It *was* for the best," Jeb said. "Everyone understood."

"Everyone except Laney."

His father stared at him for a moment, as if unsure where to go with this.

"Have you thought about all the people you're going to hurt?" Jeb asked. "The people who are parents to that child? Who've made her part of their family? Not to mention the child herself?"

Caleb glanced down, then met his father's gaze. "I keep having these dreams. About Laney. For a long time after she died, I prayed for that. To close my eyes and see her the way she was. Happy. Beautiful. But I couldn't even have her that way. And then a few weeks ago, I started dreaming about her. She's crying. Asking me why I gave away the baby. Why I didn't take care of the baby."

Tears rolled down Jeb's face and dropped onto the kitchen table. Caleb had only seen his father cry once in his life. And that was on the day of Laney's funeral.

"Then one day this woman and child walk into the store, and it's as if I've been given another chance to do the right thing. As if Laney put them there in my path so I could see."

Jeb's jaw worked, as if he were searching for words and couldn't latch on to a single one. "I don't see how anything but pain can come from this, Caleb," he finally said, his voice rough with emotion.

"I have to make peace with what I did, Dad. For Laney. And right now, there is no other way."

CATHERINE STOOD AT THE CORNER of the house, watching her son drive away, her heart breaking.

Jess, her old Australian shepherd, leaned his shoulder against her in quiet sympathy.

"Catherine?"

She walked around to the front yard where Jeb stood on the porch, his expression grim.

"You all right?" he asked.

She nodded once and sat down on the step. Jess sat next to her, his head on her lap.

"It's never going to end, is it?" Jeb said, wrinkles of defeat lining his forehead.

She looked out across the yard, set her gaze on the mailbox, biting her lip to keep from crying. "We have to be there for him, Jeb."

"With what, Catherine? How much more can you take?" He hesitated a moment, and then said, "I hear you crying in the bathroom with the shower on, Cath. I know what this has done to you, what it's doing to you. You won't let me help, and I don't see how you can be a part of something that is bound to bring even more heartbreak to everyone involved."

Catherine pressed her lips together, unable to deny anything he had said. How could she explain that she felt their son's pain as if it were part of her own skin? It had been that way since the day he'd been born, every cry, every hurtful thing that had happened to him had echoed within her as if the pain were her own. But that was what being a mother was all about. Her heart felt as bruised and battered now as it had the day they'd been called to the hospital and found their daughter-in-law in a coma.

Life had been so smooth, so good until then. She and Jeb both had loved Laney like their own daughter. Laney and Caleb had been trying to have a baby, and Catherine had looked forward to having a grandchild, her joy deepened by her own desire to hear little feet on the hardwood floors of their house.

After Caleb, she and Jeb had tried to have more children. Four miscarriages later, her doctor had warned them not to try again. She didn't think it possible to love more than she loved Caleb, but she often wished there had been brothers and sisters for him. Someone else to buffer the pain of what he'd endured these past three years. Give him the support and understanding only family can give.

He was so alone now. So unreachable. As if he'd dropped himself in the middle of the ocean, and no matter what kind of boat they used to try and rescue him, the waves around him were simply too high. She saw him drowning a little more each day, and there was nothing she could do to save him.

She rested her chin in her hand. "I'll do whatever I can to be there for him," she said softly.

Jeb stood quiet for a long time. "I wish I could say," he said finally, "that I know we'll survive this. But I don't know it. And I don't think I can stand around and watch the rest of what we once had dissolve into dust. My heart can't take it, Cath."

She looked up at him. "What are you saying, Jeb?"

He looked down, scuffed the toe of his boot against the grass. "Maybe I ought to move out for a while."

Catherine shook her head to clear the fog that seemed to have settled over her brain. "You can't mean that," she said. "We can get through this—"

"That's what I've been telling myself for three years now. But we're not getting through it, Cath. We're drowning in it." And with that, he turned and walked back into the house.

SOPHIE LEFT HER OFFICE as soon as she finished talking with Irene. She couldn't wait to get home and put her arms around her daughter.

Darcy had left the university early that day for a doctor's appointment and had offered to pick up Grace from preschool along with Will, her youngest.

When Sophie walked into her kitchen, Darcy and the two children were covered in flour, the counter dotted with cookie dough.

"We decided to do some baking," Darcy said, smiling. "Or my version of it, rather."

Sophie went straight to Grace, picked her up from the stool where she sat with dough-covered hands. She held her daughter tight, tucking her face against Grace's sweet-smelling neck.

Grace giggled and pulled back. "Hi, Mommy."

"Hi, sweetie," Sophie said, her voice uneven, forcing herself to loosen her hold. "How was your day?"

"Good. We're making peanut-butter cookies."

"They smell good," Sophie said.

"Wanna help?"

"I'd love to."

Darcy put a hand on Sophie's shoulder. "Is everything all right?" she asked carefully.

Sophie looked up, saw the worry on her friend's face, and wished she could spill the entire story of what had happened earlier. "I just really missed my little girl today."

"Mommy, can Lily have a cookie when we're done?"

The dog was stretched out on the floor by Grace's stool, as usual no more than a few inches away. "I don't see why one would hurt."

"You'll like these, Lily," Grace said, wiggling out of Sophie's embrace. "Come on, Mama. You can make your own pan."

Once they had the last of the cookies in the oven, Grace, Lily and Will went out in the backyard to play.

"Are you sure you're all right, Sophie?" Darcy asked once they were alone, concern in her voice.

Sophie pulled a Brillo pad from beneath the sink and began scrubbing the cookie sheets. She yearned to confide in Darcy, but she couldn't talk about it yet. She was afraid that if she did, it might make it more real. "I'm fine," she said. "Thanks for picking Grace up today. That was a treat for her."

"You're welcome," Darcy said, clearly not convinced. "Neal has a business thing tonight. I'm supposed to go with him, but I can hang around a while if you'd like the company."

"No. You go. Really."

Darcy hesitated and then said, "Okay. I'll talk to you tomorrow?"

Sophie nodded.

She stood at the sink for a long time after Darcy and Will had left, staring at the half-washed baking sheet. From the yard came the sounds of Lily's playful barking and Grace's resultant giggles. The soundtrack of her life now. How could she possibly live without it?

Before Grace, her life had been one of predictability. She loved her work. Enjoyed coming home at night to the classical music to which she cooked dinner and read in the double chair by the fireplace.

For someone who had grown up in a household of constant anger and yelling, this was a life to appreciate.

Since the adoption, there were those who said what a lucky child Grace was to have been given a home with Sophie. But on this, she had never agreed. She knew the truth. She had been the lucky one. *She* had been the lucky one.

CATHERINE MADE BREAD every Friday afternoon.

She'd done so for enough years that the ritual was as automatic to her as the other chores she'd made a part of her weekly schedule. Pay bills on Monday morning; laundry on Tuesdays and Thursdays; Wednesday for gardening.

Routine helped keep the heavy darkness inside her at bay. On some level, she rationalized that if she kept moving, it couldn't catch up with her. If she kept moving, she wouldn't have time to think about the growing distance between Jeb and her.

The phone rang just as she placed the first two pans in the oven. She closed the door, then picked up the phone with the hand not covered in dough.

"Catherine, it's Mary."

She immediately stiffened. Where she had once felt the deepest pity for her son's mother-in-law, Catherine could summon nothing more now than disappointment. Mary Scott blamed Caleb for everything, including the fact that he hadn't shown his grief publicly. That he refused to be interviewed by the press about what kind of person his wife had been. That he didn't visit her grave. "Hello, Mary," she said, attempting to keep her disapproval from her voice.

A heavily burdened sigh echoed across the line now. "I've heard something I cannot begin to imagine could be true."

Catherine pushed a flour-dusted hand through her hair. This phone call had been as inevitable as the end of the day; nonetheless, its arrival made her weary. "Yes, Mary?"

"I've been told that Caleb has located the child."

Catherine kept silent for a few moments,

wishing there were some way to exclude Mary, to keep her from learning about this search for redemption Caleb had undertaken. "He wasn't looking for her, but yes, he has seen her."

"I can't believe that I would have to learn something like this through gossip."

"What gossip, Mary?"

"Your husband talking to the pastor about it. His secretary told my sister, and that's how I have to find out about this? What did we ever do to Caleb that he would even think of putting us through this kind of hell?"

"Mary, this doesn't have anything to do with you," she said, surprised that Jeb would have talked to the pastor.

"Nothing to do with me!" The words came out as one long shriek.

"No. It doesn't," Catherine said, keeping her voice low and measured. "This is about Caleb's guilt over giving Laney's child away."

"Laney's child! That child was not Laney's. She did not choose to become pregnant with it."

"I understand your grief, Mary," she said, a sudden flash of anger slicing through her for a little girl she had never seen. "But you have let it turn you into someone you did not used to be."

"That's easy for you to say. You still have your son."

"Yes. Would it make you feel better if he were dead, too?"

Mary hesitated long enough that Catherine thought it would have given her comfort, indeed.

"How many years have we known each other, Catherine? I thought you were our friend. How can you allow him to do this?"

"You've pushed all your friends away," Catherine said softly. "People who genuinely wanted to help. As for my son, he is responsible for his own decisions. I have to go now. Goodbye."

Catherine hung up the phone hard enough to jar her arm, crossed the kitchen floor to stand in front of the flour-covered countertop. She stood there for a moment, her hands shaking. She plunged them into the dough and began to knead with a ferocity that had the job done in a couple of minutes.

She lifted the mound, dropped it into the greased bread pan, reshaped it a little, then set it on the stovetop to rise.

She went to the window that looked across one of the hay fields and saw Jeb on the tractor at the far end. There had been a time when the first thing she would have done was to run out and tell him about the call from Mary. It hit her with a fresh jab now that she couldn't talk to him about it. And she felt the dividing line between them widen yet again.

SOPHIE WAS IN HER OFFICE on Monday morning when the phone rang. She knew before answering what the call would be about. It was as if all her internal radar had been attuned to danger, and the warning signals pulsed through her.

The attorney was a woman. She spoke in a low, calming voice, requested a meeting at Sophie's earliest convenience. Sophie referred the woman to her own attorney and hung up, breathing deeply.

She stared at her reflection in the mirror on the wall across from the desk. The wide, fear-stricken eyes were her own. The disbelief, as well. She felt as if she'd been ambushed, a war waged against her when she hadn't even known to be afraid.

It was Sophie's nature to know the why of things. She needed to know the why of Caleb Tucker. Only then would she know which direction to take from here.

SHE BOOTED UP HER LAPTOP and logged on to her Internet connection service.

She typed in *Google.com*, waited for the search line, then keyed in *Laney Tucker.* 490 hits. Sophie clicked on the first, an article in the *Charlottesville Observer.*

The paper's logo appeared in the left-hand corner of the screen followed by a headline.

Local Woman Raped, In Coma
CHARLOTTESVILLE—A woman was abducted from the parking lot of the University Mall Tuesday night. A passerby spotted her vehicle with the driver's-side door open and a set of keys on the nearby pavement. The woman was found just after midnight Wednesday, unconscious, near a rest stop off I-64 where she had allegedly been dumped. Authorities say she appeared to have been raped and beaten.

The victim, identified as Laney Tucker, 30, of Charlottesville, is reported to be in a vegetative state and is listed in critical condition.

This is the third abduction and rape to occur within the Charlottesville city limits since January. Police would not comment as to whether the incidents are related.

Sophie stared at the words, then read through them once more, a sick feeling sweeping over her. She put her hand to her stomach, blinked hard.

Caleb's wife. Raped. In a coma.

A dozen questions raced through her mind. Among them, had she lived? And where did Grace fit into all of this?

She clicked back a screen, chose the second

Google item listed. Another article from the *Observer*, this dated several weeks later that same year.

Man Killed in Police Chase
WINCHESTER—A Charlottesville man, identified as Larry Chilinger, 38, was shot and killed after an hour-long car chase leading from Fauquier County into Winchester, Virginia, Sunday. The chase followed an attempt by police to question Chilinger regarding the rape and abduction of a Charlottesville woman, Laney Tucker, 30, last month.

Chilinger is suspected in the rape and abduction of two other women earlier this year, both from the Charlottesville area.

According to family members, Tucker has been in a persistent vegetative state since she was found unconscious outside a rest stop off I-64.

Doctors would not comment on her prognosis.

Again, Sophie read through the article a second time, a knot of disbelief sitting tight and hard in her throat.

Grace's mother. This had happened to Grace's

mother. Frantic now, she clicked back to the list of articles, chose the third listing.

An obituary flashed on the screen. Sophie sat back in her chair, put a hand to her mouth.

Laney Ashworth Tucker.

Age thirty-one. Survived by husband Caleb, parents Emmitt and Mary Scott.

Thirty-one years old.

Sophie put her hands over her face, closed her eyes as a torrent of emotion roared through her, as deafening as a spring river out of its banks.

Dear God.

How terrible. How unjust.

And how trite both words sounded. How completely ineffective at describing the horror that had led to her daughter's birth.

She recalled then the well of pain in Caleb Tucker's eyes when he'd stood in her office Friday morning. He'd made a mistake, he'd said. Grace. Born to his wife out of a nightmare. And he'd given her away. Awoken from his own coma of grief to realize what he'd done.

Dear God.

Oh, dear God.

SOPHIE PACKED UP HER BRIEFCASE and walked out of her office, one hand on the wall to support herself. Darcy appeared at the other end of the hall, waved and called out, "Hey, Sophie."

Sophie tried to respond, but the greeting came out sounding like someone else's voice.

Darcy stopped at the door. "Hey. You're white as a ghost. Is something wrong?"

"I'm all right," Sophie said, even as the walls of the building closed in around her. Any second, she would be flattened between them.

Darcy's expression said she clearly did not believe her. "Are you sure?"

Sophie nodded once and then said, "I have to go, Darc. I'm sorry."

"Sophie, wait—"

But she bolted down the hall, pushing through the doors and out into the sunshine, her lungs screaming for air.

She drove straight to Grace's preschool. She pulled up in front and got out of the car, her legs unsteady beneath her.

Inside, Greta Harper, the woman who ran the school, greeted her. "Sophie. You're early."

"Yes. Something's come up, and I have to go out of town," she said, trying to calm the breathlessness from her voice. "Would you mind getting Grace for me?"

"Of course. Will you be bringing her next Monday?"

"I don't know yet," Sophie said, biting back the urge to scream at the woman to just get her daughter. She couldn't panic. Had to remain clear-headed. But the fear cut through her. "If you could get Grace, I'm in a bit of a hurry."

Mrs. Harper nodded, curiosity in her expression. "I'll be right back," she said, without asking anything further.

A couple of minutes later, Grace came bounding through the door into the front room, Barbie lunchbox in one hand, her Blanky in the other. "Mama! You picked me up early."

"Yes," Sophie said, lifting the child into her arms, loving the solid reality of her.

"I didn't eat my lunch yet. Do you want half of my sandwich?"

"We're going to take a little trip. Maybe we can have a picnic on the way."

"Can Lily come?"

"Absolutely."

"Where are we going, Mama?"

"It's a surprise," Sophie said.

CHAPTER EIGHT

CALEB SPENT MOST OF Monday on the tractor, mowing a ten-acre spot of land he and his dad had planned to fence in the fall for new pasture.

The sun was warm on his shoulders, and for the first time in longer than he could remember, he felt rested. For the past three nights, he had slept without dreaming. Friday night in the porch rocker. And then Saturday night, tired to the bone, he'd actually climbed into bed, certain the dreams would chase him back out again. But he'd closed his eyes and slept the night through.

Last night had been the same.

And even though the rest of the world would likely think him crazy, he knew from these past three nights of dreamless sleep, he had finally found a way to give Laney the only thing left for him to give her.

Peace.

BY FIVE O'CLOCK THAT afternoon, Sophie had reached the North Carolina line. Grace was asleep in her car seat, Lily curled up next to her.

Sophie drove with a firm grip on the wheel, a headache knocking in one temple. Her glasses were in her briefcase in the back, and she hadn't wanted to take the time to stop and get them.

She drove within the speed limit even though the urge to push past it tugged hard. With every mile, the panic loosened a bit more, and by the time they reached Greensboro, Sophie finally felt as if she could breathe again.

At the house, she'd tried to stay calm when the voice in her head had screamed *HURRY!* She had to put distance between her daughter and the man who had suddenly become the enemy.

As soon as they'd pulled out of the driveway, Grace had declared them on an a'venture, sharing her PBJ with Lily when Sophie had asked if she would mind saving their picnic until they got where they were going.

They'd stopped once at a McDonald's to go to the restroom, ordering a vanilla milkshake for Grace and a cup of water for Lily.

Sophie had popped in a CD of fairy tales, which Grace had heard a dozen times, but never tired of.

At four-thirty, the cell phone had rung. She'd

glanced at the caller ID, recognizing the number for her attorney. And had let it ring.

IT WAS ALMOST ELEVEN when they reached the Myrtle Beach city limits. Grace had been asleep for the last three hours, so instead of stopping midway, Sophie had driven on. She followed the signs to the heart of the hotel strip, stopping at the first decent-looking place with a vacancy sign posted. Sophie pulled up front and rolled down her window. A bellman stood by the door.

"Excuse me."

"Yes, ma'am," he said.

"Do you allow dogs here?"

The man shook his head. "Service animals only. Try the Marley down the street to your left. Shouldn't be a problem there."

"Thank you," Sophie said.

Luckily, the Marley had its vacancy sign lit. Sophie turned into the medium-size hotel with a rush of fatigue. Her eyes were so tired she could barely keep them open. But they were here. In a place where Sophie could think. Just as soon as she got a few hours of sleep. She would think. And figure out what to do.

DELIVERIES TO TUCKER'S began at six-thirty.

By eight o'clock on Tuesday morning, Caleb

had helped unload a shipment of horse feed and another of fertilizer. The last truck had just pulled away from the loading dock when the cell phone in his pocket rang. He wiped his forehead on the sleeve of his denim shirt and reached for the phone.

"Caleb, it's Amanda." Amanda Donovan's voice held the soft politeness of an Alabama upbringing. Her manner was deceptive though. She'd never lost a case. She played to win and, in fact, this was the reason Caleb had hired her. For everyone concerned, he wanted this over quickly. Not some long, drawn-out court battle that turned all their lives into a made-for-TV movie.

"Yeah," he said.

"I called Irene Archer, Dr. Owens's attorney, yesterday afternoon to set up a meeting. I spoke with her again this morning, and it seems there's a little problem."

"Problem?"

"No one knows where she is. Apparently, she asked for a substitute to take over her classes. The department head doesn't know when she'll be back."

Caleb dropped his chin to his chest and rubbed the bridge of his nose. "So what does that mean?"

"I don't think we should do anything hasty." She hesitated and then said, "Look, clearly she's had a shock. Maybe we should just give her a little time to come to terms with this."

"And what if she's decided to leave for good and take the child with her?"

"I don't think she would do that. From what I've been able to gather about Dr. Owens, she's a levelheaded woman, well respected and liked. Let's give it a day or two, and if she doesn't show up we'll get the police to find her."

"You'll call me when you know something?"

"I will."

Caleb clicked off the phone. He stood there in the morning sun, and let himself think for a moment about what Sophie Owens must be going through. He did not want to cause her pain. That was the last thing he wanted.

But what had happened to him was unimaginable, the stuff he read in newspapers about other people.

And maybe that had been one of the hardest facts to accept. That fate could turn its scope on you, blow a hole right through every hope and dream you'd ever had, when all along you'd thought it was pointed at someone else.

He was sorry for the situation they were in. Sorry about the whole damn thing.

Because the truth was Sophie Owens was going to be another victim.

Just as he had been.

Just as Laney had been.

CATHERINE AWOKE AT daylight, but lay in bed, unable to sleep, unable to get up. A black shroud hung over her and she could no longer see through it. The blackness kept her from finding a spot of happiness in a life that had once been full of little else. Just as it kept her from helping her son find his way back to some sort of peace. And from reaching her own husband, as well, who had told her last night he was moving out this morning.

He wouldn't actually do it. She'd repeated this to herself throughout a night of little sleep. He couldn't. She felt now as if the blackness would swallow her whole, and wondered if this was what her mother had felt when she hadn't gotten out of bed for days on end.

But her mother had been different. Her mother's depression, or blues, as it was called then, had ruled her life for as long as Catherine could remember.

Catherine herself had been perfectly fine until the tragedy with Laney. And grief was normal. Why couldn't Jeb understand that?

She heard him now in the bathroom, getting ready for the day, the sounds so familiar to her. The clink of his razor on the porcelain sink. The squeak of the cabinet door, opening, closing. The whoosh of water from the faucets.

They used to get ready together, sharing the

shower, talking about their plans for the day. A piercing yearning for what they'd once had broke its way through the darkness inside her like a pinpoint of light, and for a moment, she willed herself to get up and go to her husband, make things like they used to be.

But the effort seemed more than she could manage, her legs and arms leaden with a tiredness that sleep never cured.

The bathroom door opened. Jeb stood framed in the light, handsome in a pair of crisp blue jeans and a white shirt. He didn't move for a few moments, then crossed the floor and sat down on the side of the bed, careful not to touch her.

"You awake?" he said.

She gripped the blanket with both hands. "Please don't do this, Jeb."

He stared out the bedroom window. "Oh, Cath. I can't go on like this."

In all the years they had been married, she had never once heard this awful resignation in his voice. She eased up on her elbows, smoothed a hand over her hair. "It will get better. I know it will."

"I thought so," he said, his voice quiet. "But this thing with Caleb and the child…I know what it's going to do to you. And I can't stand by and watch any longer."

She studied him, started to speak, then pressed

her lips together. When she finally found her voice, it didn't sound like her own. "I know I haven't been myself—"

He put his hand on hers and squeezed. "I would do anything in the world to help you. Take you anywhere you agreed to go. But you won't let me. And until you want to help yourself, it doesn't matter how much I want to."

She sat up straight. "Jeb. There's *nothing* wrong with me."

He stood then, his face a mask of grief. "We've been through this so many times, Cath. And nothing changes. Nothing ever changes."

"Jeb, please. Don't go."

"I love you, Catherine, but I can't watch you like this anymore. And what's happening with Caleb, how will you get through it?"

He walked to the closet and pulled a suitcase from a shelf. He threw a few pairs of pants inside, grabbed shirts, socks and underwear from the bureau drawers.

All the while, she sat watching him, dazed, disbelieving. He didn't mean it. He couldn't do this.

When he was done, he looked at her, an unbearable sadness in his expression. "I'll come by in a few days to get some more of my stuff."

"Jeb," she said, her voice breaking. "Don't. Please. Don't."

He shook his head once, then turned and walked out, closing the door behind him.

"I'm not like her!" she screamed in the silence. "There's nothing wrong with me!"

She heard the front door open, then close.

She collapsed onto the bed and wept.

SOPHIE HADN'T BOTHERED to set an alarm, and both she and Grace slept until almost nine, unheard of for either of them.

As soon as Grace opened her eyes, she leaped from the bed and ran to the window, pulling back the curtain. "Mama, we're at the ocean! It's so big!"

"Really big, isn't it?" Sophie got out of bed, swung Grace up in her arms and carried her out onto the terrace. She breathed in the potent scent of salt and sand.

"Can we go swimming in it?"

"As soon as we take Lily for a walk and get some breakfast."

"Let's hurry, Mama," Grace said.

An hour later, they were outside, and Grace was every bit as fascinated by the ocean as Sophie had been when she'd first seen it as a girl.

They rented chairs and an umbrella, building sandcastles and playing in the water. Lily ran back and forth in front of them, barking at the waves until she finally collapsed in the shade of the umbrella, exhausted.

At lunchtime, they ordered sandwiches from the hotel waitress covering their spot of beachfront and chased them down with frosty glasses of iced tea. When they'd finished eating, Grace curled up on a towel beside Lily and went to sleep, too.

Sophie sat in the lounge chair, sunglasses covering her eyes, a novel on her lap. She had yet to read a word. As wonderful as the morning had been, it was shadowed by the reality she had driven away from, but not escaped.

She could not explain why she had brought Grace here except that long ago, it seemed to Sophie like a place where a person could see the horizon in the distance, gauge the breadth and depth of problems that seemed to have no answer.

When she'd been eleven, Sophie had been invited to go to the beach with her best friend Allie's family. They'd gone every summer, Sophie's friend and her brother so used to the trip that they'd endured the seven-hour drive with bored tolerance, not interested in any of the road games their mother had kept suggesting they play. But Sophie had been so excited she hadn't slept the night before. Her aunt and uncle had never taken vacations. At first, Uncle Roy had issued a flat no to her request to go, but when Aunt Ruby had said she could do with a vacation from taking care of Sophie, he had agreed to let her. To Sophie, it was the most exciting thing she'd ever done. To earn the money for the trip, she'd cleaned out the neighbor's chicken coop every morning for two months.

She'd always wanted to go to the ocean. Listen to its sound. Taste the salt water on her lips. As soon as they'd arrived, she'd waited with pounding heart while Allie and her brother had changed into their swimsuits and complained about having to go the beach when there was a great pool at the motel. Allie's mother had insisted they take Sophie to the beach first because she had never seen it.

She'd stood at the water's edge, staring at the waves rushing onto the sand and the endless horizon. The other two children had run into the water, yelling for her to follow. She had, finally, not with the arms-wide-open abandon of her friends, but with one careful step at a time, wanting to remember each one in case she never got to come again.

The ocean had been everything she'd imagined and more. It made her feel the possibility of things, that there were places in the world for her to go, things she could be.

Sitting before that same body of water, arms folded across her chest, Sophie was exactly what she wanted to be. A mother. She had accomplished the other goals she'd set for herself. Teaching at a respected university. Making a place for herself in a community she had grown to love. And for those things, she felt satisfaction. But life had not taken on dimension, depth, until Grace.

It had been a very long time since she had chosen running as a solution to her problems. When she was younger, she'd seen it as the only way to find a new start. She'd packed what few belongings she had, left in the middle of the night and hitchhiked her way out of the hills of southwest Virginia. That seemed like someone else's life now, so long ago that memory had blurred the feelings of hopelessness.

But it was back now, filling her lungs like the batting in the hand-sewn quilts her mother had once made for her.

She breathed in the sea's fresh air. She was not the same girl she had been all those years ago.

She reached in the bag next to her chair and pulled out her cell phone. She dialed the number for voice mail. "You have eight new messages."

The first was from Irene Archer. "Sophie, please call me." Two more and then by the fourth, Sophie could hear the worry in her voice. "Sophie. I know you're upset, but we need to talk."

Two hang-ups and then another message from Irene. "Sophie." She paused. "Don't do something you'll regret, okay? We'll get you through this. It will be extremely important that we show you as the stable, competent woman you are. Call me, okay?"

The next was from Darcy. "No one seems to know where you and Grace are. Call me on my cell, okay?"

Sophie dropped the phone back into her bag, lowered her glasses and massaged the space between her eyes where a headache had suddenly appeared.

Her thoughts veered to Caleb Tucker. Something she had refused to let herself do since the phone call from Irene. She wanted to hate him. Wanted to let anger for what he was about to do burn away any sympathy she might have felt for him.

She closed her eyes and reached deep for the emotion.

It wasn't there.

Every time the anger got a foothold inside her, the words from the newspaper articles jumped into her consciousness, and her heart hurt.

Sophie stood to lose something unbelievably precious, but then Caleb Tucker already had.

They were two people who wanted the same thing. To love this child to whom they both had claim. But Sophie's claim was legal. She had done nothing wrong. He had made a decision three years ago. Surely, any judge would force him to abide by that.

Sophie had always believed in playing by the rules. Life had structure that way, made sense. She didn't know how to be any other way, even with the most important part of her life at stake.

What choice did she have but to fight for her daughter within the parameters of the law? She had right on her side. If she clung to that, then maybe she could move them both through whatever they had to face until they came out on the other side.

She pulled the phone from her bag again, walked toward the ocean, stopping where she could still hear Grace if she woke up. She punched the phone directory, scrolled through and clicked on the fifth one down. The receptionist had barely said, "Just a minute, please," before Irene came on the line.

"Sophie," she said, her voice braided with relief and panic. "Where are you?"

"I wanted to show Grace the ocean," she said, her voice soft. "It was something I've been meaning to do. Should we set up a meeting for when I get back?"

"They've asked for Friday morning," Irene said carefully. "Is that all right?"

"Yes," Sophie said. "I'll be there."

CHAPTER NINE

ON FRIDAY MORNING, Caleb pulled his truck into the parking lot outside the office of Quinn, Lewis, Day. Sophie Owens's dark blue Volvo sat a couple of spaces over. The sight of it sent a wave of tangled emotion roiling through him. But he couldn't let emotion sway him. Over the past couple of days, he'd given himself several different versions of this lecture. He was about to toss a hand grenade into the middle of someone's life, it was true. And his regret for that was genuine, actually made his bones ache.

He wished that he did not have to walk into this office and do what he was about to do. He wished that three years ago he had left the hospital with the baby that belonged to his wife. That he had not given her away to become a part of someone else's life only to arrive at this regretful day and ask for her back. But he didn't have the slightest choice. To give his wife the peace she deserved, he had to get Laney's child back.

Inside, the office was cool enough to raise chill bumps. The receptionist was a young woman with red hair and an angry-looking earring in the side of her nose. She had kind eyes, though, and he could see she already knew who he was. "I'll let everyone else know you're here," she said, picking up the phone and announcing his arrival to the person on the other end.

She stood and said, "Follow me, sir."

The hallway was long and narrow, lined with heavily framed prints of foxhunting scenes. They followed it to the end where she opened a door and said, "Right here, Mr. Tucker."

"Thank you."

Amanda Donovan sat alone in the room. Dressed in a stern pin-striped black suit with a white blouse, she fit the image of a no-nonsense attorney. She stood and said, "Caleb. Good morning."

"Morning," he said.

"Irene and Dr. Owens should be right in. Coffee?"

He shook his head. "I just want to get this over with."

No sooner had he said the words than the door opened again, and Sophie Owens stepped into the room, followed by an older woman with soft gray hair secured in a loose knot on the top of her head.

"Good morning, Mr. Tucker," she said with a

polite nod. "I'm Irene Archer. You've met Dr. Owens, of course. Everyone, please sit down."

Caleb nodded at Sophie. He'd intended to look away. But the look of barely concealed terror in her eyes made his stomach drop.

She wore a navy dress with a short strand of pearls at her throat, its very simplicity making her seem vulnerable compared to the dressed-to-intimidate attorneys in the room.

He waited for the three women to take their chairs, then pulled out his own and sat, settling his gaze on the yellow legal pad in front of him and his thoughts on what he had come here to accomplish.

The receptionist offered coffee. They all declined.

"Well," Irene Archer said. "I think the purpose of this meeting is to simply get everything out on the table. Ms. Donovan?"

Amanda tapped a yellow pencil on the tabletop. She glanced at Caleb. "Clearly, the circumstances of this meeting are regrettable. My client has no desire to bring pain and suffering to Dr. Owens. He is also extremely grateful for her care of the child in question over these past three years. But after much painful consideration, Mr. Tucker is contesting the grounds of the adoption based on the extreme duress under which his decision to give up the child was made."

A small sound came from Sophie Owens's

parted lips. Irene reached over and put a hand on top of hers.

Caleb's gaze lifted to Sophie's. The terror had been replaced with tears. He could see that she had expected the words, prepared herself for them, and yet how could a person prepare for being told someone wanted to take away her child?

Her child. He looked away.

"Mr. Tucker." Irene cleared her throat. "I am aware of the circumstances surrounding your decision to give up Grace Owens. And I am deeply sorry for all the pain you have endured. But I must ask you, in pursuing this decision, are you aware of the devastation you will bring to Dr. Owens's life and to the child in question, as well?"

Caleb met the attorney's disapproving stare. "I can assure you, Ms. Archer, that none of this is what I would choose if I felt that I had a choice."

"I have to tell you then that my client will take this to the highest court who will hear our case. It will be a very long, drawn-out and ugly dispute. Is that what you really want?"

"No, it's not what I want," he said. "But it's something I have to do."

"Very well, then. We had hoped you would have had a change of heart, Mr. Tucker. Since that doesn't seem to be the case, we will see you in court."

She stood then, put a hand on her client's

shoulder. Sophie got to her feet as well, her expression dazed and slightly unfocused. Caleb wanted to say something, but could think of nothing that seemed appropriate.

"Are you all right?" Amanda asked when the door had closed behind them.

Caleb nodded, got to his feet too quickly, his chair teetering behind him, then righting itself and hitting the floor with a loud thump. "Is that all for today?"

"Yes. I'll have a word with Irene before I leave. I'll be in touch, Caleb."

He left the office then, went outside and stood for a moment on the brick walkway, letting the sun warm his chilled skin. But it did not reach the frozen knot that had lodged in his chest.

He headed for the truck, but came up short halfway across the parking lot. Sophie Owens sat in her car, one arm draped over the steering wheel. Her shoulders shook, and he could hear her sobs through the rolled-up window.

He stood frozen by her grief. Grief he had created. He told himself to leave her alone. That he was the cause of this. That he should walk away.

But conscience or empathy or something he wasn't willing to put a label on urged him forward. He tapped on the glass with the back of his fingers, lightly enough so that if she didn't hear him, he could tell himself he had tried.

She jerked her head up, her eyes wild with emotion she'd somehow managed to control in the attorney's office just a few minutes before.

He made a motion for her to roll down the window.

She shook her head and waved him away.

He knocked again. "Please."

She turned the key, pushed the window button and lowered it halfway.

"Are you all right?" he asked.

"Fine," she said, her voice sounding as if its normally smooth edges had been abraded with sandpaper.

"You shouldn't drive like this."

"I'm fine," she said again and began to raise the window.

He put his hand on top of the glass. She let off the button. "I'm sorry," he said, the words quiet, inadequate. "I know you don't deserve this."

She looked up at him, fresh tears filling her eyes. "But that's not going to stop any of it, is it?"

The question filled the air between them, and he sensed her silent but palpable pleading for him to change his mind. To make all of this go away.

"I'm sorry," he said. It was all he could find to say.

SOPHIE STOPPED AT A SANDWICH place a few blocks from the law office, went to the bathroom and washed her face with cold water, using a harsh brown paper towel to pat it dry. She stared at herself in the mirror. The last few days had taken their toll.

She looked as if she'd aged ten years since leaving the house this morning. Her lids were red and puffy. Dark circles had appeared beneath her eyes. She looked bruised and beaten. Felt as if her deepest layer of muscle had been pounded with a hammer. How foolish she had been to hope. And yet she had been hopeful. Prayed that Caleb Tucker's heart would change, that he would decide against tearing Grace's life to shreds.

But that was exactly what he was going to do.

She gripped the edges of the sink and bent forward, her hair slipping partially free from the pins securing it. The pain was like being immersed in liquid fire, and she was unable even to swim to the top and gasp for air. Sophie was Grace's mother. *Her mother.* And she could do nothing to prevent what was going to happen to her child.

She straightened, seeing in the mirror the truth in her own eyes. Had she been able to turn back the clock, she would have given up her opportunity at motherhood to spare Grace this. But she possessed no such magic wand. She tossed the paper towel in the trash can. It was time to do what she should have already done.

CATHERINE HEARD THE KNOCK and considered not answering it.

She lay on the couch, the living room's closed shades and drawn curtains blocking the sunlight. She turned over, pressed her face to the lavender-scented pillow she'd brought down from her bedroom. These past few nights, she'd slept here, unable to face sleeping alone in the bed she and Jeb had shared for more than half her life.

"Mom?"

At the sound of Caleb's voice, Catherine jerked up from the sofa, fumbled with the switch on an end-table lamp. She blinked against the light and smoothed a hand across hair that hadn't been brushed in days. She didn't want him to see her like this. "Just a minute," she called out.

"Where are you?"

She got to her feet, a wave of light-headedness washing over her. "In here," she said.

Caleb appeared in the doorway, a worried look on his face. "Are you all right, Mom?"

"I— Yes," she said, tightening the belt of her robe. "Just a little under the weather."

He came into the room, his gaze taking in the closed curtains. "Have you been to the doctor?"

"No. It's nothing like that. I'll be all right in a day or two."

"Where's Dad?" he asked.

Catherine bit her lip and glanced down, considering how to answer. "I'm not sure."

Caleb was silent for a moment, and then said, "What's going on, Mom?"

She looked up at him, then sank back down onto the couch, all the energy suddenly draining from her. She pressed one hand to the pounding in her temple. "Your father… We've separated, Caleb," she said finally, unable to find any way to soften it.

"What?" he asked, staring at her, as if he couldn't quite process what she'd said.

"He moved out a few days ago."

Caleb shook his head. "Why?"

"Oh, son. It's complicated."

"But the two of you…he's crazy about you, Mom."

"Things change. People change," she said, the words little more than a whisper.

"There has to be a reason."

"He's been unhappy," she said, hoping he wouldn't press her for a more specific answer.

"Unhappy," he said, the word now laced with anger. "What the hell does that mean?"

"Caleb—"

"Mom, this is ridiculous. He can't just leave you."

"Son, this is between your father and me. I don't want you to—"

"It's not just between you and him," Caleb interrupted, slamming a palm against the door frame. "Damn him."

"Don't, Caleb," she said, her eyes welling with tears.

"Where is he, Mom?"

She stared at her son for a few moments, too tired to deny him the answer. She knew him well enough to know he'd find out one way or another. "He left an address on the kitchen table."

"Are you all right, Mom?"

"I'm fine," she said. "Really."

Caleb backed up a step. "I'm going to see him."

"Caleb, please. Don't."

"I'll be back to check on you later," he said, then left.

CALEB GRIPPED the steering wheel, his knuckles white. He didn't believe this. His father had never been the kind of man who would even think about leaving his wife. What was going on?

He took route 29 into Charlottesville, then drove around for a few minutes looking for the apartment building on May Street. His father's truck was parked outside, and he took the stairs to the second floor, knocking on the door marked 10.

He waited a minute or two, and when there was no answer, knocked again. He heard footsteps, and then the door opened. At the sight of his dad,

Caleb blinked hard. Jeb's face was drawn and haggard, his eyes red, from lack of sleep or crying, Caleb wasn't sure.

"Hello, son," Jeb said, his voice drained of its former energy.

"What's going on, Dad?" Caleb asked, shaking his head.

Jeb stared at him for a moment, then said, "This is between me and your mama, son."

"Yeah, that's what she said. Both of you look absolutely miserable."

Jeb glanced away, then met Caleb's gaze again, not saying anything.

"I don't understand how you can do this to her," Caleb said, the anger he had tamped down on the way over rising to the surface again. "You love her."

"Sometimes, that's not enough, son."

Caleb jerked a hand through his hair. "Do you have any idea what you're throwing away? What you're going to lose if you don't turn this around?"

"I know exactly what I'm losing," Jeb said, the response low and sad. "But the truth is I already lost it."

"What are you talking about, Dad? I know Mom doesn't want this."

"Caleb." Jeb glanced down at his hands. "Things aren't like they used to be."

"So you just throw away all those years you've had together?"

"It's not what I want, son."

"Then why are you doing it?" Caleb asked. "How can you be so selfish? Is there someone else? Are you screwing around on—"

"That's enough," Jeb said, the words out on a flash of heat. "You have no idea what you're talking about."

"Really?" Caleb asked, his own voice thick with disgust. "Why else would you turn both your lives inside out?"

Jeb stared at him, then looked away.

"At least answer that."

When Jeb remained silent, Caleb backed up. "I have no idea who you are," he said.

Caleb had reached the stairs when his father's voice rang out in the hallway. "I'm not the one who's changed."

Caleb waited.

"You know, son, I would have taken your suffering onto myself if I could have," he said. "I'd give anything I have to prevent you from going through these past three years. But I can't. I can't take it away. Even if I could, you wouldn't let me. You're punishing yourself, Caleb. And I don't think you're ever going to stop. Watching you do this to yourself has just about done your mother in. I can't stand by and watch her refuse to get help any longer."

Caleb felt as if his father had hit him in the chest with a hammer. He stood there, disbelieving. "So everything that's happening between the two of you is my fault?"

"That's not what I said."

"I think it's exactly what you said," he snapped. "And you know what, Dad? I'm not buying it."

He took the stairs down two at a time, got in his truck and sped out of the parking lot, wishing he'd never come in the first place.

JEB STOOD AT THE APARTMENT door long after the sound of Caleb's truck faded.

Had he said too much? Been unfair?

He ran a hand around the back of his neck. He couldn't answer yes to either question. He loved his son. But he thought what he was doing was wrong. And he couldn't pretend otherwise.

These past few days without Catherine had been the worst days of his life. Getting up in the morning just seemed like a waste of time, because without her there was no light.

A dozen times, he'd pulled his suitcase out of the bedroom closet, told himself he couldn't take another moment away from her.

But then nothing had changed. As long as Catherine refused to get help, he couldn't bring himself to go back and watch her slip further from his grasp.

A panicked urge to go after his son hit him dead center, but just as quickly dissolved.

Caleb had made up his mind. Nothing Jeb said was going to change it. And he couldn't bring himself to resume his position on the sidelines where he could only bear witness to the wreckage.

CALEB DROVE HOME FASTER than he should have.

He rapped a thumb against the steering wheel in rapid staccato. So it was his fault. *He* was to blame for the problems in his parents' marriage. *He* was the reason his father had moved out. *He* was the reason everything around him had fallen apart these past three years.

He wheeled the truck into his driveway, spewing dust behind him on the gravel road. At the house, he stomped the brake, skidded to a stop.

He opened the door, but didn't get out. How the hell had he become the villain?

Anger coursed through him, and in its wake, a wash of refusal to take responsibility for this. His father's decision to leave was his own. And if he chose to break his wife's heart, then the choice was his. There was nothing Caleb could do to stop it.

CHAPTER TEN

THAT NIGHT AFTER FINISHING Grace's bath, Sophie tucked her daughter into bed, then sat down beside her, smoothing the back of her fingers across the child's silky blond bangs. She smelled sweetly of Johnson's baby shampoo.

Lily lay at the foot of the bed, already curled up asleep.

"Aren't you going to read to me tonight, Mama?"

"I thought we might talk for a little bit instead. There's something I need to explain to you, honey."

Grace reached for Blanky and pulled it up beside her. "What, Mama?"

Sophie tipped Grace's chin up to look deep into her eyes. "This is not something that will be easy for you to understand, but you know how much I love you, don't you?"

"As much as the sky is wide," Grace said, repeating one of the answers Sophie always gave whenever her daughter asked her that question.

"That's right. And that will never, ever change."

Sophie bit her lip. "You didn't come into my life the way some babies do."

Grace frowned. "I didn't come out of your tummy like Jenny's new baby brother?"

Sophie shook her head. "No. You came from a very special place. A family who decided when you were born that another mommy could take better care of you than they could. And so they gave you to me because I wanted you so much."

Grace looked down at her yellow blanket, rubbing her thumb across its ragged silk edge. "You needed me?"

"Yes, sweetie. More than I could ever say."

"Was my other mama sad?"

Sophie's throat tightened, and she swallowed deeply. "I'm sure she was very sad."

"Does this mean I'm adopted like Alina?"

"Yes, baby, it does." Alina was in Grace's play-group. She had been adopted from Russia as an infant, and her parents had been open with her about it from the beginning. Sophie wished now that she had done the same with Grace. She wondered what it was that had held her back, some sense of unease she could not even explain.

"Will I ever see my other mama?"

"No, baby." Sophie hesitated, and then forced herself to say the words. "But she had other family who have decided they want to know you."

Grace rubbed the edge of the blanket again, and Sophie could see her measuring her thoughts. "So I'll meet them?"

"I think so," Sophie said, swallowing past the knot of despair inside her throat.

"Will you be with me?"

"There will be a judge involved who will tell us all how that's going to work. We'll have to wait and see what the judge says."

Grace frowned, her lower lip quivering. "Mommy, I'm scared."

The grief inside Sophie broke free then, and tears wet her face. She pulled back the covers, got in bed beside her daughter and pulled her into the circle of her arms. "I know. But we'll get through all of this together. Everything is going to be all right."

"Promise?" Grace asked, her voice small.

Sophie closed her eyes, knowing she had no way of seeing into the future, of defining what "all right" would be. "I promise," she said. Because somehow, some way, it just had to be.

TWO WEEKS LATER, Sophie parked her car in the lot next to the courthouse and sat for a moment, reaching for courage, calm, but finding little of either within grasp.

Grace had not brought up the subject of being

adopted since the night Sophie had tried to explain everything to her. Selfish though she knew it to be, she was glad because it allowed her to close that door in her own mind, except for the times when she was alone and the terror roared over her, deafening, numbing.

Inside the courthouse, Sophie took the elevator to the fourth floor, followed the numbers to the end of the hall. A window looked out onto a side lawn. An older woman stood just outside the door. Caleb's mother. Their resemblance clear. She looked to be in her midfifties, pretty still in a way few women were at that age. Her gaze met Sophie's. The compassion in the woman's eyes sent a knife of pain through Sophie's side, and she ducked into the courtroom.

Irene waited for her up front. On the other side of the aisle sat Caleb Tucker and his attorney. He looked up, met Sophie's gaze, and maybe it was only her imagination, but she thought he looked as sorry to be here as she was. But then he had instigated the proceeding, and it was fully within his power to stop it.

Irene put a hand on Sophie's shoulder as she let her take the seat farthest from the aisle. "Good morning," she said. "How are you?"

"Okay," Sophie said.

The courtroom door opened, and she glanced

back to see the woman from outside take a seat. Sophie faced forward, clasping her hands in her lap.

Irene leaned over. "Ida Hartley is the judge assigned to our case. We could have done worse."

Judge Hartley entered the chamber then, taking her seat behind the enormous podium at the front of the room. Streaks of gray threaded her dark brown hair. Rectangular glasses sat perched on the end of her nose. She glanced at a folder in front of her, then said, "Would counsel please approach the bench?"

Both attorneys stood and walked over. The judge spoke quietly with them for a minute or two, nodding once, then frowning before they returned to their seats.

"Good morning, Mr. Tucker. Dr. Owens." Judge Hartley gave a polite nod to them both. "Am I to understand then that Mr. Tucker desires to disrupt the adoption of Grace Owens, the three-year-old girl adopted by Dr. Owens?"

Amanda Donovan stood. "That is correct, Your Honor," she said, her voice quietly respectful.

Judge Hartley said nothing for several moments. "I will be honest with all of you," she finally said. "I am saddened by the nature of this request. As much as it goes against my own personal feeling that once finalized, an adoption should be exactly that, I will hear your arguments with the clear and unbiased application of our laws as my guide in deciding on this matter. If I might ask a question or two of you first, Mr. Tucker?"

Caleb stood and said, "Yes, Your Honor?"

Sophie looked at him then, unable to keep her gaze from straying to the grim lines of his face. His jaw was set, his hands anchored on the edge of the table in front of him.

"I am aware of the very unfortunate circumstances influencing your decision to give up your late wife's child three years ago," Judge Hartley said. "What has happened to change your mind about the wisdom of that decision?"

Sophie turned her gaze to the judge, forcing herself not to look at Caleb.

He cleared his throat. "I have no words to explain my grief over my wife's death. I'm not even sure how I lived through it. But I do know that I was in no state of mind to make the decision I made. And I realize now that it is not what my wife would have wanted. I am only asking that the court give that consideration."

"I assume, Mr. Tucker," Judge Hartley said, "you understand the gravity of what you are about to do."

He didn't answer right away, the silence in the room thick and expectant. "Yes, Your Honor."

The judge's nod was grave. "Very well then. Dr. Owens."

Sophie stood.

"I have reviewed the social worker's reports of each of her visits to your home since the adoption. It is clear you've met every expectation for an adoptive parent and then some. And that, in my eyes, makes this situation all the more regrettable."

Sophie pressed her lips together and laced her fingers together tightly.

"Do you understand then that Mr. Tucker will be asking this court to reverse the adoption? To remove Grace Owens from your home and place her in his?"

The words echoed within her like rifle shots. She nodded. "Yes, Your Honor. If I might add something?"

Judge Hartley gave a single nod of permission.

"While it's true that my own world is being turned upside down, my concern is for my daughter. I've tried to explain to her a little of what is happening, but she's only three. How can she possibly understand this? I'm the only mother she has ever known."

The judge picked up the papers in front of her and restacked them with a quick motion. "This is a most undesirable situation in which to put a child, and I would advise both parties," she said, looking from Sophie to Caleb, "to keep this little girl's well-being first and foremost in whatever requests are made of this court.

"We will adjourn then and reconvene—" she paused to glance at her calendar "—two weeks from today. Same time. Is that acceptable with counsel?"

Both attorneys agreed by saying, "Yes, Your Honor."

Judge Hartley stood then and left the courtroom.

Irene squeezed Sophie's arm. "Are you all right?"

"Yes," Sophie said. "But I really need to get out of here."

"Go. I'll be in touch," Irene said.

Sophie pushed her chair back and followed the center aisle out of the courtroom without glancing again in Caleb Tucker's direction. Even so, she felt his gaze on her back, and it was all she could do to stop herself from begging him not to do this.

Outside the courtroom, she pushed the button for the elevator, willing it to hurry. The courtroom door swished open again.

"Excuse me."

Sophie turned.

The woman Sophie had seen here in the hall earlier stood with her hands clasped in front of her. "I'm Catherine Tucker," she said, her voice not quite steady. "Caleb's mother."

Sophie drew in a half breath, caught off guard by the woman's directness. "Yes."

"I just wanted to say—" She stopped, rubbed

her right hand against the fabric of her navy blazer. "I really have no idea what to say. I just wanted you to know that my son doesn't wish to bring you deliberate pain."

"I'm afraid it's already too late for that."

"I expect it is."

Sophie considered the words and then said, "I understand what your family has been through. And I am more sorry than I can say. But a decision was made three years ago that was thought to be in the best interest of my daughter. I can't see how tearing her away from the only life she knows now can be in her best interest."

"My son…Caleb…he can't seem to let go of what happened. It's as if it has a grip on his soul, and to be honest, there are times when I think it will pull him under completely. He thinks he wronged Laney by giving up the child. He has horrible dreams—" She stopped then, as if she thought she'd said too much. She glanced down, sighed heavily, and then looked at Sophie. "I just wanted you to know there's no malice toward you in any of this."

The older woman turned to go back into the courtroom.

"Mrs. Tucker?" Sophie called after her.

She looked back. "Yes?"

"I have no intention of giving her up."

Catherine Tucker was quiet for a moment, and then said, "You don't appear to me to be the kind of woman who would."

The elevator dinged. Sophie stepped inside, the doors closing behind her.

CALEB FELT LIKE HELL and looked worse.

For the past few days he'd had a migraine headache that had kept him locked in a dark room for thirty-six hours. Only by Friday morning had it softened to a dull roar.

He forced himself out of the house behind a pair of dark sunglasses, his bloodstream struggling to process a maximum dosage of Advil.

Since the meeting in front of Judge Hartley, Caleb had tried to go about his normal life, forcing his thoughts away from the course of events he had set into motion.

But it was as if someone had tied a two-hundred-pound weight to his ankle, and he struggled for every inch of forward movement.

The whole thing had been far worse than he'd ever imagined. Or maybe that was just it. He'd never thought it would feel as if he were personally leading Sophie Owens to her own execution.

And then the day after the hearing, the reporters had started calling. He'd deflected three of them so far, but he knew how they worked. If he refused to play, they'd write what they wanted to write anyway.

Caleb drove to the store with a cup of coffee in one hand, Noah on the other side of the seat with his head out the window.

It was early still, not quite seven, but Macy was already at the counter putting cash in the register when he walked through the door.

"Morning," he said.

She looked up at him, then quickly dropped her gaze. "Good morning."

"Something wrong?"

Macy sighed once, reached beneath the counter and pulled out a newspaper, handing it to him. "Sorry, Caleb."

He glanced at the front page and read the headline. Adoption Contested.

His stomach dropped.

Without glancing at it further, he went upstairs to his office, closed the door and sat down at his desk.

The words glared out at him. And suddenly, he was in the middle of it all again. Saw the lights of Sheriff Overby's car swing into his driveway when he'd been expecting Laney. Heard the sorrow in the older man's voice when he took off his hat and said he had some bad news to deliver.

He forced himself to read the article start to

finish. It was like immersing himself in acid, peeling back skin and sinew until there was nothing left to eat into but bone.

Noah came up the stairs, nudged the door open, crossed the office with wagging tail and put his head on Caleb's knee. He made a short whining sound, his dark eyes questioning.

Noah had always had a sixth sense for detecting distress. Whenever Laney had been upset about something, the world wasn't right for Noah until he felt she was okay.

Caleb rubbed the top of the dog's head, pierced by a knife of loneliness that cut so deep he thought he could never possibly be whole again. "It'll be all right," he said, wishing he could believe it.

SOPHIE DROPPED GRACE OFF at preschool and then came home to find the headline shouting from the front page of the *Observer*. The phone had been ringing nearly nonstop for the past hour while she sat at the kitchen table, unable to make herself get up and continue the day.

The doorbell brought her out of her daze. She considered ignoring it, too, but pulled herself out of her chair and walked to the living room, spotting Darcy's minivan in the driveway. She opened the door knowing that she could no longer hide what was happening.

Darcy stood with the paper in her hand. "My God, Sophie. Why didn't you tell me?"

Sophie shook her head, bit her lip. "I kept thinking it couldn't come to this. That if I didn't talk about it, it would go away."

Darcy stepped inside, closed the door, then pulled Sophie into her arms. "Oh, Sophie. I'm so sorry."

A sob broke free from Sophie's throat. They stood that way for a long time, embracing one another, neither of them holding back their tears. Sophie finally stepped away and said, "It wasn't that I didn't want to tell you, Darc. I just couldn't."

Darcy smoothed a hand over Sophie's hair. "I'm your friend. I will be here for you in whatever way you need me to be. Starting now."

Sophie nodded once and squeezed Darcy's hand. "Thank you," she said. "I think I'm going to need you."

ON MONDAY MORNING, Sophie's attorney called and asked her to come by that afternoon to go over a list of questions. The weekend had been a somber one with Sophie trying to pretend everything was normal, amid concerned phone calls from fellow professors and teachers at Grace's preschool.

That afternoon, Sophie drove downtown to

Irene's office. The receptionist sent her right in, Irene herself barely visible behind the mound of files on her desk.

"Could I get you anything?" she asked, standing up, her assessing gaze sweeping Sophie's face as if looking for evidence of how she was holding up.

"No, thanks. And I'm okay, Irene. I'm not going to fall apart."

"No one would blame you if you did," Irene said, sitting down again in her black leather chair. "It's going to be all right, Sophie. We've just got to come up with our game plan and then follow it to the letter."

Sophie sat up straighter. "So what is the plan?"

"Show the judge what an incredible parent you are. What an incredible life Grace has. And how absolutely unthinkable it would be to take that away from her when it is all she knows."

Sophie nodded, reassured somewhat by the quiet conviction in Irene's voice.

"We'll start with pictures of the house," Irene went on, "Grace's room, play area, her dog, her day school. We need a visual representation of the life you two lead. I want to lay it all out for the judge to see."

"Will my being a single parent be a negative in her eyes?"

"It shouldn't be. But we're going to have to build a convincing case. Admittedly, Mr. Tucker has the sympathy factor on his side."

To Sophie, the words sounded as if they were preparing for some enormous chess game, each seeking to outmaneuver the other.

"And your extended family," Irene said. "We'll need pictures of them, too. Grandparents, aunts, uncles—"

"I only have an aunt and uncle," she said carefully. "They really haven't been involved in Grace's life."

Irene sat back in her chair. "Hmm."

"Will that be a problem?"

"Maybe. It would be beneficial to have relatives who can vouch for you as a mother."

"I have friends, coworkers."

Irene considered this for several moments. "Sophie, I think it would be extremely helpful if we had at least one relative to stand up for you. I don't know how to say this in a way that doesn't scare you to death, so I'll just put it straight out. We need every ounce of ammunition we can get. Even this particular detail could make or break our case."

A little while later, Sophie drove home well under the speed limit, still dazed by Irene's last statement.

She had not spoken to Ruby or Roy since Grace's birthday party, and she'd realized that the only reason they'd come had been to convince her to sign over something that had belonged to her mother.

But what was pride when faced with losing her daughter? Grace was all that mattered now.

And for her sake, Sophie had no choice but to ask for her aunt and uncle's help, difficult though it would be.

CHAPTER ELEVEN

On the following Friday, Sophie packed the car and headed down I-81, her heart beating faster with every passing minute of the four-hour drive to Hubbard Springs, the small town tucked into a corner of southwest Virginia where she had grown up.

From her car seat in the back, Grace sang along to the CD of children's music Sophie had brought with them. Her happy little voice squeezed at Sophie's heart, and she prayed that Grace's joy for life would not be diminished by this nightmare she felt she had less and less control over.

She took the exit off I-81 and drove toward the center of town. Fifteen years and little was different. Another fast-food restaurant or two. Signs that had sprung up by the side of the road like stray weeds, bold and abundant.

She drove to the west side of town, then took a secondary road to the section of the county where her aunt and uncle lived. The house was medium-size, a brick ranch-style surrounded by a neighborhood of others exactly like it, save for different colors of trim. A burgundy minivan sat in the driveway.

The front door of the house opened. Ruby stepped outside.

Sophie got out of the car, the urge to pull away from the curb and leave as strong as it had been so many years ago when she actually had left. She lifted Grace from her car seat, queasiness now making her legs weak, and walked up the driveway, stopping just short of the minivan. "Hello, Aunt Ruby."

"Unless you're here to sign those papers," the older woman said, her tone dismissive, "we have nothing to say to one another."

"Could we go inside?"

Ruby said nothing, simply turned and headed for the door. Sophie followed, old feelings of rejection pummeling through her.

Not much inside the house had changed. The lighting still dim behind tightly drawn curtains, polyurethane wood floors shined to a mirror gloss. A long narrow table covered with family photos sat just beyond the foyer. There wasn't a picture of Sophie anywhere among them.

In the living room, Sophie set Grace on the couch, placed a LeapPad on her lap and told her she wouldn't be long. "Could we go in the kitchen?" she asked Ruby.

Without answering, Ruby led the way, turning on the faucet and filling the same teakettle that had sat on the stove for the duration of Sophie's childhood.

"I'm a little surprised you'd have the nerve to come back here," Ruby said, the condemnation behind the statement barely contained.

Sophie pressed her lips together and then said, "Aunt Ruby, I didn't come here to talk about the past."

"So why did you?"

"I need your help," Sophie said, her voice low.

The silence was heavy. "It's always been about your needs, hasn't it?"

Sophie flinched beneath the harsh unfairness of the words. There would be no changing her aunt's perception of why Sophie had left here. She wouldn't even bother to try. "It's about Grace. The man who signed away his rights to her wants her back. I have to go to court."

For the briefest second, Sophie thought she saw sympathy in her aunt's eyes. But she turned her back and picked up the whistling kettle from the stove. "What is it you want?"

"My attorney says it's important to have a family member testify for me."

"I think you've written us off as anything close to that, don't you?"

Sophie let the accusation go, focusing on the sole reason she had come. "If you could be there, it might make the difference between my keeping her or losing her."

"Funny how we think we can cut our ties, turn our backs and walk away, but family is always family, isn't it? You never know when you'll need each other."

Accusation underlined every single word, but Sophie said nothing, just waited, her gaze level with her aunt's.

Finally, Ruby turned away again and poured the hot water over the tea bags. "I tell you what. You give me what I want. And I'll give you what you want. Sign your mother's part of the land over to me, and we have a deal."

Sophie stared at her aunt's back, then said softly, "It must have been awful for you."

Ruby turned to look at her. "What?"

"Having to raise me."

She lifted a shoulder. "I did what was expected of me."

"An obligation."

"Would you rather I candy coat the truth and tell you it made our lives easier? That we had the things we wanted because of you?"

Sophie let the words settle, a sadness she had long ago locked away inside herself rising to the surface.

"Aunt Ruby. I was a child. The only thing I ever wanted from you was love. And I guess the truth is that was the only thing you could never give me."

Sophie reached for the purse she had set on the kitchen table, pulled out the papers Ruby had left with her when they'd come to Charlottesville. She scrawled her signature across the bottom of both pages, refolded them and handed them over. "Here. You have what you want now. The hearing is Wednesday at ten o'clock. My attorney has asked if you can come to her office the day before to go over some questions."

Ruby glanced at the papers in her hand. "I'll need a hotel room then," she said.

"I'll take care of it."

Sophie went into the living room and picked Grace up from the couch. She walked to the front door, then turned. Ruby stood in the hallway, arms folded across her chest. "And you don't have to worry after this, Aunt Ruby. Be assured this is the last thing I will ever ask of you."

GRACE SLEPT DURING MOST of the drive home, her head resting against the side of her car seat, a toy giraffe clutched in one hand. Every time Sophie glanced at her innocent face in the rearview mirror, fear washed over her in a dizzying wave.

Despite the fact that she had agreed to ask for her

aunt's help, she didn't see how Ruby could change any of this for them. Regardless of how glowing a picture she painted of Sophie as a mother.

The truth? There was only one person who could stop the horror that had taken over Sophie's life. And there had to be some way she could make him see.

IT WAS NEARLY DARK on Sunday night by the time Caleb finished his barn work and went inside the house. He took his boots off and headed with little enthusiasm to the kitchen, Noah trailing behind him with a stuffed bear in his mouth.

Caleb had filled every minute of the past few days with work, anything to keep himself from thinking too far past his own exhaustion.

He opened the refrigerator door and stared at the nearly empty shelves. A half-full bottle of ketchup. Gallon of milk, date still good. Two sticks of butter. Eggs.

He pulled out the carton of eggs, the few slices of bacon left in the Tupperware container, set a frying pan on the stove and sprayed it with PAM.

The bacon had just started to sizzle when a flash of light arced through the kitchen from the front windows of the house. A minute later, there was a knock. Thinking it might be his mom, Caleb stuck his head around the kitchen doorway and called out, "Come on in."

The door swung open. Sophie Owens stood framed against the night with a bundle of photo albums in her arms.

Surprise smacked Caleb in the chest. He could think of nothing to say.

"I should have called first," she said. "But I thought you might think it was a bad idea for me to come."

He stared at her for a moment. "Sounds like it might be."

She hugged the albums tighter to her chest and said, "I won't take up too much of your time. May I come in for a few minutes?"

The smell of burning bacon reminded him of the pan he'd left on the stove. "My dinner," he said and headed back to the kitchen. She followed him.

Noah got up from his spot under the table and trotted over to greet her, tail wagging.

Sophie reached down to rub the dog's head.

Caleb dumped the burned bacon in the sink, shot another glance at the woman still rubbing his dog. Her hair was pulled in a ponytail at the back of her neck. The color wasn't blond, and it wasn't brown, but fell somewhere in between the two, nondescript but for its shine. He gazed just to the left of her and said, "Why are you here?"

She put the albums on the table. "I wondered if you might look at these."

Caleb knew what she was asking him to do, knew also that he would be better off telling her no. But she looked vulnerable, and it must have taken a decent amount of courage to come here tonight. He couldn't find it in him to ask her to go.

So he pulled out a chair and sat down at the table, opening the first of the albums.

A soft breeze stirred through the open kitchen window. The smell of green grass drifted through, and it was the first time in a long while that he could remember appreciating the scent.

The pictures were dated with little captions written in calligraphy beneath each, the obvious effort of someone who never wanted to forget the details of the events captured there.

The first was of a smiling Sophie—a look of clear incredulity in her eyes—holding a tiny infant whose mouth made an O of outrage. Caleb felt a jolt of pain for the fact that the baby pictured in Sophie's arms had so recently left his wife's womb. He had chosen not to see her the day of her birth. What would have happened if he had? Would his heart have softened? Could he have seen past his rage to the needs of that baby?

He turned the pages, one by one, reading each caption. *Grace's first day at home. Grace's favorite blanket. Me with Grace on her first stroller ride in the park.*

While he immersed himself in the album, he was aware of the woman in his kitchen moving quietly across the room to the stove. At the sound of bacon sizzling in the pan, he looked up. "You don't have to do that," he said.

She shrugged. "It'll keep my hands busy."

The protest inside him dissolved as quickly as it had risen. He went back to the albums, still aware of her putting the bacon on the plate he'd set out earlier, then cracking eggs into the pan. She went to the front porch, Noah on her heels, returned with a handful of something green, rinsed it in the sink, then minced it into pieces and threw it in with the eggs, adding salt and pepper from the shakers on the counter.

A few minutes later, she brought the plate over and set it beside him, a fork wrapped inside a napkin.

"Thank you," he said, looking up at her, caught off guard by sincere appreciation for her effort. "Have you eaten?"

"Yes. Go ahead, please."

The bacon was perfectly cooked, and she'd found a couple of pieces of bread to toast and butter. The eggs were good, too, the herb she'd thrown in—parsley?—adding an interesting layer of taste. Laney had planted the herbs when she'd become interested in cooking, but Caleb had been tempted to pull them up when they returned each spring even though she was no longer here to care for them. He was glad now that he hadn't, glad that Sophie had noticed them, given them purpose again. He ate everything on the plate, actually wished for more. "Thank you," he said.

"You're welcome." She smiled in a way that reminded him how nice it was to have another human being in his house. A woman in his house. Watching her, fresh pebbles of remorse scattered through him.

He put his attention back on the second album, opening the cover to what must have been Grace's first Christmas. She sat in one of those baby swings a short distance from the tree, looking up at the star on top with wide-eyed delight. Her face was beset with pure joy, and Caleb was struck still, wondering whether she would have had that look had he brought her home as his own. With only grief and misery in his heart, how could he have introduced a child to anything so selfless as joy?

It was a sobering thought. His hand slowed at turning the pages. And suddenly he couldn't look anymore. He slid his chair from the table, got up and went out into the yard.

He stood in the dew-soaked grass, dropped his head back, breathed in deep and hard.

Behind him, the screen door squeaked open. How long had he been meaning to fix that hinge? Like so many things on this place, he just hadn't found the energy or the will to get to it.

"Are you all right?"

Her voice held a note of concern, and uncertainty as well, as if she weren't sure whether she should have followed him out. "I'm fine," he said, wishing she hadn't.

She came out into the yard, stopping just short of him. "I didn't mean to upset you."

"If your intention was to make me see that I could not have given Grace the life you've given her, then you were successful."

"That wasn't my intention." Her voice was soft, sympathetic.

At that, he balked. He did not need this woman's pity. He was tired of being pitied. Sick of being poor Caleb Tucker, what-a-shame-things-had-to-turn-out-that-way. "So what was it then?" he asked, the edge of the question sharp.

"To humanize myself in your eyes," she said, throwing up her hands in a burst of emotion. "Show you that I'm not just some name on the court docket opposite yours! This is my life! My daughter's life! And what you are about to do—" She broke off there, struggling for composure. "What you are about to do…please," she said. "I beg you. Don't."

She swung around then, ran up the steps and through the screen door. A few moments later, he heard a car start. And as unexpectedly as she had arrived, Sophie Owens was gone.

CATHERINE LIVED FOR Jeb's visits to the farm.

He never came in the house, just went to the barn, completed the list of chores she could not do alone and then left again, as silently as he had arrived.

Each day, she watched him from the kitchen window, and even though he was only a hundred yards away, he felt distant and unreachable to her.

This morning, the sun stood high in the sky. The day would be a hot one. She watched while Jeb backed the big John Deere tractor out of its shed, a mower attached to the back. She opened the cabinet beneath the kitchen sink and saw the water Thermos Jeb always took with him when he was mowing.

Before she could talk herself out of it, she put it under the tap, filled it to the rim, then carried it outside.

Jeb had just started toward the field at the back of the barn when he spotted her. He stopped the tractor and turned off the engine.

She held up the Thermos. "I thought you might want this."

He jumped down, landing on the ground with

the grace of a much younger man. "Thanks," he said, taking it from her and setting it beside the tractor seat. "I'll need that today."

She nodded and folded her arms across her chest, suddenly too conscious of her uncombed hair, her lack of makeup. "Do you have your phone?" she asked, the words out before she remembered maybe it was no longer her place to worry about him.

He patted the side pocket of his Levi's. "Got it."

She glanced down at the grass beneath her feet, biting her lip. "Jeb—"

"How are you, Catherine?" he asked before she could finish.

She looked up and saw the sincere interest in his eyes. "Okay," she said, even though she was anything but. "How about you?"

"Fine," he said.

They stood there, staring at one another. It seemed unfathomable to Catherine that after all their years together, they could find nothing to say.

"You've seen Caleb," Jeb said finally.

"He comes by every day."

"Good. He's pretty angry with me."

Unable to deny it, Catherine said nothing.

"Is he all right?" Jeb asked.

"As much as he can be, I think," she said.

Jeb inclined his head, regret clear in his expression. "He came to see me after he found out about us."

"I didn't ask him to do that."

"I know," he said. "I doubt he'll ever forgive me."

For several long moments, they stood, silent. There was so much she wanted to say. Pride had long ago deserted her. Suddenly, she didn't think she could stand one more lonely night without her husband. "Come back, Jeb."

"Catherine," he said, pain etched in his voice. "If I thought things would be different—"

"They will be," she said, putting a hand on his arm, hopeful that she had finally reached him. "I promise they will be."

He looked at her for several moments. "You'll see a doctor then?"

The words hit her like a cold splash of water. She took a step back. "I don't need a doctor," she said. "I'm fine. Can't you see that?"

He glanced at the house where the shades were drawn on every window except for the kitchen, where she had observed his visits. His gaze settled on her again. She put a hand to her hair, remembering then that she hadn't washed it in days. Glanced down at the khaki pants and white blouse she'd fallen asleep in last night and hadn't bothered to change this morning.

"Catherine," he began, then stopped and turned

toward the tractor. "I'm sorry," he said, not facing her. "I'm sorry."

He turned the key and the engine growled to life. She stood in the same spot, watching him drive across the field, smoothing a hand across her wrinkled pants. He didn't believe her. And for the first time, she didn't blame him. It was a lie. All a lie. She no longer believed herself.

THE NEXT WEEK PASSED as if someone had put life on fast-forward.

Sophie tried not to listen for the phone, tried to tell herself not to hope that Caleb might have a change of heart and call this whole thing off.

Wednesday arrived with no such call, and she dressed for the hearing with hands that shook to the point she could barely button the white blouse she'd chosen to wear under her navy suit.

Darcy arrived at the house just before eight, having agreed to stay with Grace while Sophie was gone. Somehow, she didn't want to take her to preschool today, wanted her to be with someone who could remind her that Mama would be home soon.

After setting Grace up at the table with her bowl of Cheerios, Sophie leaned over and kissed the top of her silky hair, lingering a moment longer than normal.

"Be a good girl today?"

"I will, Mama."

Darcy put a hand on Sophie's shoulder, her eyes brimming with tears.

"I'd better get going," Sophie said, willing herself not to cry in front of Grace.

Darcy followed Sophie to the front door. "Are you sure you're all right?"

"I'm okay."

"Come here," Darcy said, pulling her into her arms and hugging her hard. "I'll be thinking about you every minute."

Sophie bit her lip, nodded and then hurried out to the car. Inside, with the doors closed, the tears came, and she cried all the way to the courthouse because she simply could not help it.

So, CLEARLY, SHE HAD BEEN wrong to hope that her visit to Caleb's house might have made a difference.

Any softening she might have seen in him that night was gone this morning, in its place the same expressionless mask he had worn before.

His mother again sat in the back of the court-room, alone. Sophie sat next to her attorney, glancing over her shoulder at the door a dozen times before it finally opened, and her aunt and uncle walked through.

Ruby wore a red dress with black buttons up the

front. Her hair had the marks of a recent perm, her nails painted a bright crimson. Next to her, Uncle Roy looked less certain, as if he weren't at all sure why they were here. His shoulders weren't as straight as they had once been. He dropped his gaze to the hat in his hand. Aunt Ruby had a grim expression on her face.

Irene had called late yesterday afternoon to say she had met with the two of them. They'd gone over what questions she planned to ask them, and Irene had assured Sophie that everything would go smoothly.

They took a seat midway back, neither of them looking Sophie's way. A stray barb of loneliness struck her, and it seemed particularly ironic considering that the only family she had in the world, aside from Grace, was here in the courtroom with her.

Sophie straightened her spine against her chair and refocused her energy on getting through this morning. Seconds would form minutes. Minutes would inch into hours. She could do this. There had been other difficult moments in her life. Other times when she had been alone. She would get through this on her own.

She always had.

THE HEARING BEGAN PROMPTLY at ten o'clock with the entrance of Judge Hartley into the courtroom.

Everyone stood, and the judge took her seat behind
the bench without looking at either Sophie or
Caleb. She called both attorneys up front, spoke
to them in tones low enough that no one else could
hear and then nodded once in dismissal.

Both attorneys returned to their seats.

"These proceedings will begin with Mr.
Tucker's attorney," Judge Hartley said. "I would
like to hear Mr. Tucker's side of this. I understand
he has declined the opportunity for a character
witness to speak for him. Once Ms. Donovan is
finished with Mr. Tucker, Ms. Archer will proceed
with Dr. Owens's character witness and then Dr.
Owens herself. That will comprise the first part of
this hearing. Ms. Donovan?"

Amanda Donovan stood and said, "Thank you,
Your Honor. I would like to call Caleb Tucker to
the stand."

"Proceed," the judge said with a nod.

Caleb stood, walked to the witness chair, raised
his hand to be sworn in. Sophie's eyes were drawn
to his face, now set.

"Could you please tell us about your wife's
death, Mr. Tucker?" Ms. Donovan asked.

At this, Sophie's gaze returned to his face and
something inside her clenched tight with dread. He
was silent for a few moments, as if reaching for
strength. When he spoke, he was matter-of-fact.

"She had been to the mall to buy a birthday present," he said. "A man broke into her car and hid in the backseat. He abducted her."

"And what happened after that, Mr. Tucker?"

Several minutes passed before he answered, his voice thick with emotion when he finally did. "My wife was raped. And beaten."

"And she was found where?"

"Behind a Dumpster. At an interstate rest stop."

"I'm sorry, Mr. Tucker," Ms. Donovan said, looking as if she regretted the questions she had to ask. "I know this is difficult."

Caleb did not acknowledge the words, but sat stone still, his jaw visibly locked, as if willing himself through each moment.

"What happened after your wife was found?"

"She was alive. But not conscious. She never came to."

"And a few weeks later, the doctors discovered your wife was pregnant."

"Yes."

"With your child, Mr. Tucker?"

The courtroom had gone completely still.

"No," he said.

"And how was this ascertained?"

"Eventually, by blood work."

"The child your wife carried was the result of the rape?"

"Yes."

"Was abortion an option?"

He shook his head. "My wife would never have had an abortion. She had very strong views against it."

"And so your wife was kept on life support to allow the child in question to be born?"

Caleb nodded.

"If you could please speak for the record, Mr. Tucker," Judge Hartley said, her voice soft.

"Yes. The doctors gave us no hope of her recovery. When the baby was close to full term, they performed a cesarean."

"The child born was a little girl?"

"Yes."

"And you chose to put the baby up for adoption?"

"Yes."

"Can you tell us why, Mr. Tucker?"

Again, he didn't answer for several long moments. "I don't know that I can put into words the place I was in after what happened to Laney. She was my wife. I loved her." He stopped, drew in a ragged breath, and then said, "To lose her that way… I wasn't sure that I could go on living myself."

Caleb's attorney stood silent, letting the words settle over the courtroom. "And why have you now changed your mind about that decision, Mr. Tucker?"

"Because I believe I didn't do the right thing by my wife."

"Could you explain that?"

He looked down and then lifted his head, setting his gaze on some distant point at the back of the courtroom. "When Laney died, I couldn't see past the very next moment."

"I think, clearly, anyone here can understand that, Mr. Tucker. But your decision to put your wife's child up for adoption has impacted other lives, including the child herself."

"That's true," Caleb said. "There is nothing right about any of this. Not about what happened to Laney. Not what happened to the child she gave birth to or to Dr. Owens, who adopted her."

"What do you have to offer this child, Mr. Tucker?"

"A connection to her mother," he said. "A life in the place where her mother would have wanted her to grow up."

"Would your wife have loved this child, Mr. Tucker?"

"Yes, she would have," he said without hesitation.

"How do you know that?"

"Because I knew my wife. For her, the child would be innocent."

Caleb's gaze swung to Sophie for the first time since he'd begun speaking, and she was sure his eyes softened.

She glanced away, sudden emotion rocking through her. *Don't cry. Not here. Not now.* She began praying for strength.

Ms. Donovan continued. "And you harbor no ill feelings, Mr. Tucker, about the fact that you are not the child's biological father?"

"No," he said. "Laney's child is innocent. She is innocent."

"Thank you, Mr. Tucker. I have no more questions."

Caleb returned to his seat. He glanced at Sophie, and in that moment when their gazes met, it was as if the two of them were on a boat in the middle of the sea, swamping waves all around. Though she couldn't explain it, she had the feeling he would have saved them both if he could.

CHAPTER TWELVE

IRENE ARCHER, Sophie's attorney, stood and called as her first witness Ruby Murphy.

Ruby walked straight-backed to the front of the courtroom and took the stand with an air of long sufferance. She never glanced at Sophie but focused her gaze on Irene and kept it there. "If I might just ask you a few questions, Mrs. Owens."

Ruby nodded. "Yes."

"Sophie Angle Owens is your niece. Is that correct?"

"Yes, Sophie is my niece."

"And Sophie came to live with you at what age?"

"She was eight."

"And why was that?"

"Her parents were killed."

"And how were they related to you?"

"Sophie's mother was my sister."

"Did Sophie have any siblings?"

"One. Jenny. She was killed with her parents."

The words pinged at the cap Sophie had long

ago placed on memories of her family. She never let herself think of them. It was as if they had belonged to someone else's life. A sharp sense of loss cut through her now. A scorching rush of pain left in its wake blisters of regret and a sharply etched memory of her mother standing at the kitchen sink. Singing as she worked, throwing smiles at Sophie where she sat at the kitchen table stringing green beans from their summer garden.

"And you were Sophie's only remaining family?"

"Yes."

"Could you tell us, please, what kind of child Sophie was?"

"Quiet. She usually preferred books to our company."

To Sophie's ears, the disapproval rang out clearly, even though her aunt's words were delivered with a half smile.

"Dr. Owens endured a great deal of loss early in her life, then?"

"Yes, I suppose she did."

Again, Sophie heard the grudging acknowledgment in the admission, tempered as it was with the tone she remembered too well. *This world's not an easy place, Sophie. Don't think you're the only one with a cross to bear.*

Such words were the closest Ruby had ever

come to consoling Sophie over the loss of her parents and sister. And when Uncle Roy—undemonstrative as he was—might have put a reassuring hand to her shoulder, it was always pulled back at Ruby's quick criticism. "She doesn't need your babying, Roy. What she needs is to quit feeling sorry for herself."

Ruby cleared her throat now and continued. "As a child, Sophie said she never wanted to be a mother."

Irene glanced up from her notepad, clearly surprised by the comment. "And why was that?" she asked carefully.

"Before her death, Sophie's mother, Sarah, was not the most—" Ruby paused, looking as if she were searching for a palatable word. "Consistent mother."

To Sophie, the statement was baldly mocking. Again said with a soft auntlike smile, but it was impossible to miss the edge beneath. Irene frowned, piercing her witness with a dagger glare. "And your point, Mrs. Owens?"

"My point is that, surprisingly, Sophie did decide to be a mother. And I'm glad that Sarah's lack of mothering skills didn't carry over to her daughter. I tried very hard to be a good role model for her."

Sophie swallowed, pinching the palm of her left hand until the pain distracted her from the hurt that exploded inside her. This, then, was why her aunt had agreed to come here today. How could Sophie have been such a fool? Had she thought anything had changed? That Ruby might have softened her heart for the niece she had never wanted? Whose presence she'd resented every day of Sophie's life in her house?

All these years, she must have hoped for a way to pay Sophie back for what she considered her lack of gratitude for giving her a place to live. Sophie could not call it a home, because to her, it had never been one.

"That will be all, Mrs. Owens," Irene said, her expression blank.

Ruby made her way back to her seat without once looking in Sophie's direction. She heard Irene call her name, stood and made her way to the stand as if pulled by invisible strings. She answered all of the basic questions—name, place of birth, age, occupation. Numbness had removed the life from her voice, and she heard the robotlike lack of emotion in her responses. Irene's steady gaze held its own silent message: forget what you've just heard and speak from your heart.

Sophie put her thoughts on Grace, blanked from her mind Ruby's painful vitriol.

"Tell us about your daughter," Irene said.

Sophie pressed her lips together, and then said,

"I used to imagine what it would be like to have a child. And I think a lot of what I expected is actually true. But there were so many things I had no way of knowing. How wonderful it is to hear 'I love you, Mommy,' every night when I put her to bed. How amazing it is to see her gently pick up a moth from the sidewalk and put it under a bush where she thinks it will be safe. How rewarding it is to see her learning how to do things, swim, climb the ladder to her playhouse. With Grace, I feel like I've been given a chance to see the world with new eyes. She has been an incredible blessing to me."

"I have one question for you, Dr. Owens," Irene said. "Could you please tell this court why you think Grace should remain in your custody?"

It was a question with no easy answer. Sophie glanced down at her intertwined hands and then lifted her gaze to the center of the room. "I did not give birth to my daughter. But I'm the person she asks to blow on her boo-boos, the one she asks to hold her when she's tired. I'm the one who knows she likes her toast cut in triangles instead of rectangles, that she likes grape jelly but not strawberry. I know she can't go to sleep at night without the scrap of a blanket she calls Blanky. These are the things that make up her world. I did not give birth to her, but I am the only mother she has ever known, and while I understand Mr. Tucker's re-thinking of his decision to give her up for adoption, I believe with all my heart that Grace should remain with me."

Irene nodded. "Thank you, Dr. Owens."

"You may step down, Dr. Owens," Judge Hartley said.

Sophie returned to her seat and clasped her shaking hands in her lap.

"We will adjourn for lunch and reconvene at two o'clock." Judge Hartley stood then and left the room.

Sophie glanced over her shoulder. Her aunt and uncle had already gone. Of course they had not waited for her.

IRENE TOOK HER to a little place near the courthouse where most of the attorneys ate lunch. Sophie ordered a salad, which she didn't eat. Irene ordered a sandwich and did equally poor justice to it.

Sophie didn't need to ask to know she was worried.

THEY RETURNED to the courthouse at a quarter to two. The fifteen minutes before the judge returned to the courtroom seemed like fifteen days.

Sophie sat straight in her chair, as if by

forcing herself rigid, she might prevent her world from toppling.

A door opened. Judge Hartley swept into the room. Everyone stood.

She indicated that they should sit, her expression grave. "It is this kind of case that makes my job as a judge at times less than ideal. There is nothing black and white here. Many lives are involved that will be damaged in some way by the action of this court. It is my sincerest desire to minimize that damage to the extent that I possibly can. With that in mind, I am going to postpone further testimony and take a less than traditional approach to this very complicated situation."

Sophie dug her nails into the palm of her hand, praying the same prayer she had been repeating over and over all morning. *Please, dear God. Please don't take her from me.*

"Clearly, there will be no winners here," Judge Hartley said. "I should hope both you, Dr. Owens, and you, Mr. Tucker, realize that. I would there-fore like to put the weight of this problem on the two of you. I am convinced that Mr. Tucker's decision to put the child up for adoption was made during a period of overwhelming grief, and I am also convinced that Dr. Owens has been a loving mother to Grace Owens, despite the somewhat re-grettable testimony of her aunt."

The judge was silent for a moment, before saying, "I am assigning a period of time during which Mr. Tucker will be given visits with Grace. These visits should occur once per week for no less than two days per visit. We will follow this schedule for sixty days and then reconvene here in this courtroom at which time I would like to hear what both of you feel is in the best interest of this child."

Sophie squeezed her eyes shut, not sure whether she should cry or breathe a sigh of relief.

WITH THE JUDGE'S FINAL words, Amanda Donovan mouthed a quiet, pleased, "Yes." She put a hand on Caleb's arm and gave it a firm squeeze.

For Caleb, each of these things barely registered.

He should be pleased. This was a step toward fixing the mistake he'd made. And yet there was no pleasure in the moment.

He let himself look at Sophie Owens then. She sat straight in the chair but with her head tipped forward, one hand latched to the heavy wood table in front of her, as if without that anchor she might capsize.

Her attorney bent toward her, speaking quietly, the palm of one hand at the center of her client's back.

He stood then, the back of his chair banging the divider wall behind him.

"Caleb. Are you all right?" Amanda asked.

"I have to go," he said.

"I'll call you." Her words reached him halfway down the room's center aisle.

Caleb cleared the courtroom in a few lengthy strides. His mother called out to him, but he couldn't stop, couldn't face her now.

The elevator doors were open, and he bolted across the hall, jumping inside.

At the back of the elevator stood Sophie's aunt and uncle.

The aunt smiled at him as if they had just completed some successful joint venture. She looked as if she might pull a bottle of champagne from her oversize purse and pop the cork right there.

"Congratulations, Mr. Tucker," she said.

Something in her voice stuck to his skin like honey, sickeningly sweet. "I don't think there were any winners here today, ma'am."

Her penciled-in eyebrows lifted. "Really? My guess is that you'll end up with the child. You got what you came for, didn't you?"

Caleb let his gaze settle fully on her then. It was impossible to miss the satisfaction in those chilly eyes. The uncle standing next to her cleared his throat, shifted from one booted foot to the other. Clearly, Ruby Owens's intent on that stand this morning had been to settle a score. "I might ask the same of you, Mrs. Owens."

The elevator stopped two floors from ground level, the doors sliding open. A man in a suit stepped inside.

Caleb got out and took the stairs.

SOPHIE MADE HER WAY to the parking lot as if she were on autopilot, hardly aware of the steps that led her there. Her car sat in the far corner of the lot. A minivan backed out of a space several yards ahead and pulled toward her.

Uncle Roy and Aunt Ruby. Sophie raised a hand and asked them to stop. Roy did so, lowering the driver's-side window, not quite meeting her eyes.

She stared at them for a moment, and then said, "You must hate me."

"Don't be ridiculous," Ruby said, leaning across the seat, her lips a thin line of disapproval.

She shook her head. "How else could you have done that?"

"I simply told the truth."

"You wanted them to believe I don't have what it takes to be a good mother."

"You chose to believe what you wanted, Sophie. Regardless of anything I said."

"I feel sorry for you, Ruby. That you've carried that around all these years."

"You always saw everything as being about you."

Sophie gasped with the unfairness of the accusation. She had been a child in Ruby's house. A child who had lost both parents and a sister.

Roy started to say something, stopped as if thinking better of it, then spoke. "Be quiet, Ruby. I think you've done enough damage for one day." He glanced at Sophie. "I'm sorry."

His eyes held the truth of that, and in his voice, she heard apology, not only for this day, but for the whole thing. For the first time, Sophie realized that Roy did not feel the same as Ruby. Maybe his going along with her had been about keeping peace in a life that was anything but peaceful.

She wished that he could have been different. That he had stood up to Ruby a long time ago. But he hadn't. And would probably pay dearly for the stance he had taken just now.

He nodded once, raised the window and drove away.

SOPHIE LET HERSELF into the house, dropping her keys on the foyer table. Darcy came down from upstairs. "You're back," she said. "Grace is asleep. I just put her down a few minutes ago...." She stopped there, her voice trailing off.

Sophie met her friend's concerned gaze.

"Oh, Sophie," Darcy said, shaking her head.

With those two words, Sophie began to cry.

Darcy stepped forward and wrapped her arms around her. "No," she said. "No."

They stood there, holding one another up while anguish gripped them both, and Sophie tried to imagine how she would ever get through this.

THE FRIDAY MORNING marking the beginning of Judge Hartley's custody assignment arrived, weighted with a sky of heavy gray clouds.

Sophie had tried to explain to Grace, days ago, what was going to happen, that she would be spending some time with the man who belonged to Noah. She had been excited about that part at first, but now that the morning had arrived, she was subdued, not eating her breakfast, clinging to Sophie's side, as if afraid to let her out of her sight. She clutched Blanky in one hand and had started sucking her thumb, a comfort ritual she had given up at least a year before.

Sophie tried to act normal, sound normal, going about their morning routine as if nothing extraordinary were about to happen. But she heard the difference in her own voice, a note of fear that she hid from Grace no better than she hid it from herself. Finally, she picked Grace up, went into the living room and sat in the rocker by the window, holding the child close against her. Lily lay down on the floor beside them, not taking her eyes off Grace. They sat that way, until the sound of a car turning into the driveway made Sophie stiffen. She kissed Grace's forehead and said, "There's something I want you to remember no matter what. You are the best thing that ever happened to me. I love you. Nothing is going to change that. Promise me you'll remember that?"

"I don't want to go, Mama."

Sophie smoothed a piece of Grace's blond hair from her face. "Everything is going to be all right. Just different. We'll make this work, okay?"

"Mama, don't make me go," Grace said, her voice rising. "I'll be good. I promise."

"Oh, baby." Sophie's own voice broke. "You haven't done anything wrong. You're the best little girl I could ever have hoped for."

"Then why do I have to go away?"

On Grace's face, Sophie saw hurt and confusion. How could she make her daughter understand that this wasn't punishment? When that was exactly what it felt like?

She went to the door with Grace's arms wrapped around her neck, her legs around her waist, face tucked against Sophie's chest. The little girl sobbed as if her heart had broken in half.

Sophie prayed for strength, prayed for her knees not to buckle beneath the pull of her own grief.

She opened the door. A small-framed woman in khaki pants and a navy blazer greeted her with the solemnity of someone who deeply regretted what she was about to do.

"Good morning. I'm Carey Jones," she said. "I'll be taking Grace to Mr. Tucker's house."

"Her things are here in this bag. And please make sure she has her blanket." Sophie's voice was ragged as she added, "She can't sleep without it."

"I'll make sure."

Sophie hugged her daughter as tightly as she dared, wanting every ounce of her love to go with her out that door, carry her through these next two days.

The woman waited, and then said quietly, "May I take her now, Dr. Owens?"

Sophie pressed her face against Grace's hair, squeezing the child hard against her. Tears ran down her cheeks, and she didn't bother to try and stop them now. She kissed Grace's forehead and said, "Be a good girl, okay?"

Grace clung tighter, her sobs heavy and heart wrenching.

Mrs. Jones reached for her, and Sophie had to pry Grace's hands from her shoulders, telling her everything was going to be all right.

The social worker took her quickly, reaching

for the suitcase and then hurrying down the sidewalk to the car.

Grace screamed, arching her back against the woman's arm. "Mama! Maaa-maaaa!"

The sound put a permanent crack in Sophie's heart, the pain so real it took the breath from her. Lily ran back and forth in the foyer, whining.

The woman put Grace in the car seat, then got in the front and started the engine.

Sophie stood at the door, one hand covering her mouth, not sure how she would live through the next moment.

Mrs. Jones backed out of the driveway, and still Sophie could hear Grace's wail.

The car disappeared down the street. Sophie closed the door, dropped to her knees and wept.

CHAPTER THIRTEEN

CALEB WAITED IN THE KITCHEN with his mother. They'd drunk more coffee than was logical, and they were each so tense that every sound plucked at their already raw nerves.

"You're going to wear a hole in that floor, Caleb," Catherine chastised.

She had dressed in her Sunday best, but looked as if she hadn't slept last night, worry lines prominent on her face.

Just when Caleb thought he couldn't stand another minute, a car pulled up in the driveway. His mom stood. Caleb forced his legs to move him to the front door. His heart was beating so fast he could feel the pounding in his temple.

He heard the child's crying before he opened the door.

On his porch stood a solemn woman holding the little girl who sobbed a single word. "Mama." Her eyes were red and tear-swollen, and Caleb's heart caved at the sight of her.

He swallowed, and the woman said, "Mr. Tucker? I'm Carrie Jones with Social Services. Grace is very upset. I haven't been able to console her. If I could bring her inside?"

Caleb nodded and stepped back. His mother stood to the side, visibly torn by the child's wrenching cries. Caleb led the way to the living room where Mrs. Jones set Grace down, one hand on her shoulder.

Grace ran to the corner of the living room, scooted behind the oversize chair, her sobs on the verge of hysteria.

Mrs. Jones wiped a hand across her forehead. "She'll be all right?"

Caleb nodded, having no idea whether she would or not. He had never heard such heartbrokenness.

Mrs. Jones went back to the car, returned with Grace's things and then left without saying another word.

The sound of the child's anguish filled the room.

"Oh, Caleb," Catherine said, one hand going to her mouth.

Noah trotted in, having sneaked through the door from the front porch as the social worker was leaving. He went straight to the chair, ducking behind it even as Caleb started to call him back. The dog's tail thumped back and forth between the wall and the chair. Grace's crying softened to sniffles.

Caleb and Catherine stood like statues, until Noah backed away from the chair and threw a questioning look at Caleb.

Catherine crossed the room, pulled the chair out and lifted Grace into her arms. "Oh, honey," she said. "I'm so sorry. You're going to be fine. I promise."

Grace looked at Catherine, then Caleb, her lower lip still quivering uncontrollably.

"You're exhausted, aren't you?" Catherine said, smoothing a hand over the child's blond hair. "Why don't we show you your room upstairs?"

Grace looked down at Noah.

"Noah can come with us," Catherine said.

That seemed to soothe her enough to still her trembling mouth for a moment.

"I'll carry her upstairs, Mom."

Catherine started to hand Grace to him, but the child shrank away and began crying again.

"It's all right," Catherine said.

The room was at the end of the upstairs hallway. Laney had painted it a year or so after they'd been married in the hope that they would soon use the room as a nursery. The walls were a buttery yellow, adorned with nothing more than a single mirror above a small white dresser and a twin-size bed that looked lost in the large room.

Caleb and his mom had spent half of yesterday

in Toys "R" Us looking for things Grace might like. Caleb had been clueless but for the age recommendations on the boxes. Catherine had been a little more adept, picking out a soft, cuddly doll and an oversize stuffed gorilla, which now sat in the corner of the room, a silly smile on its face.

Catherine lowered Grace to the edge of the bed. "There you go, honey."

Grace shot a longing glance at the gorilla, then crawled to the head of the bed, curling up on the pillow in a fetal position. Her thumb went to her mouth, soft snuffling noises replacing the sobbing from earlier, as if she were too worn out to manage more.

Catherine looked at Caleb, pity filling her eyes with tears.

Caleb's own throat locked suddenly, and they stood there under a cloud of knowledge that there was nothing they could do to take the child's pain away. And yet, he knew, too, he was the one responsible for it.

In a few moments, the snuffling eased, and Grace's eyes closed. Noah dropped to the floor beside the bed, clearly intent on standing guard until she woke again.

Catherine pointed at the hallway and they quietly left the room, leaving the door cracked so they could hear her if she called out.

Downstairs, Caleb went to the window and looked out across the yard. "I'm sorry to put you through this, Mom."

"She's heartbroken, Caleb."

He shoved his hands in his pockets, grappling for his own belief in what he was about to say. "Things will get better. Everything is new."

Catherine moved to the window beside him, pulled a tissue from her pocket and wiped her eyes. "Do you really think this is what Laney would have wanted, son?" she asked, her voice low and hushed. "That child is innocent. More a victim than any of us. Her life has just been torn apart. It seems so unfair, Caleb."

He said nothing. He couldn't deny the truth behind her words.

"Caleb?" His mother put a hand on his arm. "I know you've wanted someone to pay for what happened to Laney. God knows we all did. But please don't let it be this child. Promise me that."

Caleb stepped back as if she had just slapped him. "Is that what you think?"

"By taking that little girl from the only mother she has ever known, you *are* punishing her, whether you mean to or not."

Caleb flinched, then ran a hand across his face. "So you've teamed up with Dad now, huh?"

"That's not fair."

"What is?" he asked.

"Caleb—"

"Maybe you should go, Mom," he said and turned away from her.

Long after she had disappeared down the gravel drive, he felt the sting of his mother's words. He went upstairs and looked in on Grace, finding her curled up in the same position asleep, Noah still on the floor beside her.

Back downstairs, he went from kitchen to living room, creating things to do that didn't need doing. His mother's accusation, however well-meant, had hit some sensitive spot inside him. Was he looking for someone to punish? Had he picked this child as his target?

Was he doing this for himself after all? On some level, had he grouped this little girl into the same category as the man who had taken his wife's life?

It was an ugly thought, and Caleb shied from it, certain only that he would never consciously hurt Grace.

But God help him if he ever laid even an ounce of his own need for revenge at the feet of that child.

God help him.

FOR AN HOUR AFTER the social worker had left with Grace, Sophie put herself on autopilot. Placed the breakfast dishes in the dishwasher, dumped the coffee grounds, set the trash out back. With every motion, her arms and legs grew heavier until she finally forced herself up the stairs, her steps like that of an old woman.

The phone rang, Darcy's cell number flashing on caller ID. She had called the day before to say her grandmother had died. She and Neal had driven to Tennessee that night to help with the funeral arrangements, Darcy upset that she could not be there for Sophie.

Sophie let the phone ring, certain she could not bring herself to talk about what had happened this morning.

She collapsed, instead, onto her unmade bed, staring up at the ceiling and wishing for some switch to pull within herself that would stop the pain gnawing away at her.

There were sleeping pills in the medicine cabinet, a prescription written for her after some minor surgery a few years ago when she'd been unable to sleep. The bottle beckoned now like a light at the end of a pitch dark road. She pictured exactly where it was on the shelf, behind the bottle of Centrum vitamins.

What would it hurt to take one?

If she could have just an hour without this awful pain, one hour, maybe she could begin to think clearly again. She got up and went into the bath-room, opened the cabinet door, reached for the bottle and stared at it.

She turned the lid, tipped the edge to the palm of her hand and shook out one tablet. The ache inside her was so all-encompassing that the pill felt like a single raindrop hitting parched earth. She shook out another.

She reached for the glass by the sink, then turned on the tap and tossed the pills to the back of her throat.

GRACE SLEPT FOR SEVERAL HOURS.

Caleb stuck his head in her room, saw that she was awake, but curled up in a ball still, thumb in her mouth, tears sliding from the corners of her eyes.

He stood as if glued to the wood floor, immo-bilized by his own ineptitude. Her body language alone said, *Stay there, I don't want you to come closer.* So he stayed where he was. "Grace?"

She shook her head and continued to look at the pillow, as if his voice were more than she could handle. He stepped back. Noah stayed at the door beside him. "I know you must be very sad right now. But everything will be all right. Will you believe me on that?"

She didn't raise her eyes from the pillowcase. "Mama," she said.

The word was so pitiful, so replete with meaning that Caleb's heart twisted into a tight knot.

Beside him, Noah whined.

Caleb put his hand on the dog's head and said, "Okay."

Noah trotted over to the bed, licked Grace's cheek, then sat with his eyes trained on her tiny face, waiting for any sign of response.

There was none. Noah whined again, as frustrated by the desire to reach her as Caleb was.

He glanced at his watch. Already midafternoon. Way past time for lunch.

Should he stay here or try to take her downstairs for something to eat? He didn't want to upset her further, and yet, they had the weekend ahead of them. He had to feed her. They would have to start somewhere.

He crossed the floor, keeping his body posture as unintimidating as he could. He squatted by the bed, his kneecaps hitting the side of the mattress. "Would you like to go downstairs and get some lunch, Grace? I understand peanut butter and jelly is your favorite."

She shook her head again. Her tears began to build in momentum. "Mama. Mama."

The walls of the house seemed to sway with the sound of the child's grief. The crack in Caleb's heart widened, and he saw himself as he must look to her. A man who had taken her from her mother. The truth hit him hard. And wasn't it so? Because to her, he was nothing more than exactly that.

IT WAS NEARLY FIVE O'CLOCK when Caleb pulled into Sophie Owens's driveway.

Grace sat in her car seat in the backseat of the truck, Noah on the floorboard beneath her. Only now did her sad face transform with happiness.

She had cried for the remainder of the afternoon, until her eyes were swollen and she could barely catch her breath. Nothing he said could console her.

Finally, he'd gathered her up, put her in the truck and driven her home.

Sophie's car sat in the driveway and lamplight shone from the living-room window.

"Mama," Grace said and began trying to unfasten the buckle to her car seat.

Caleb got out and opened the back door. It took him a few seconds to unclasp the belt. He lifted her out, set her on the ground beside him and told Noah to wait in the truck.

They headed across the yard, and Grace offered no resistance when Caleb reached for her small hand.

At the front door, he knocked. A minute passed with no answer. He rang the bell. Still no answer. Maybe she was out back.

He leaned over and picked Grace up, surprised now to find that she didn't pull away from him, then walked around the house. No sign of anyone out there.

He tried the front door again, but still no response.

He went back to the truck, reached for his cell phone and dialed the number she had left inside Grace's suitcase.

The phone rang and rang, and he began to get a worried feeling in the bottom of his stomach.

They walked back to the front door where he knocked again.

Grace pointed at the flowerpot on the top step. "Key."

Caleb bent down, lifted the edge and pulled it out. "Thank you," he said and then wondered if he should just leave and come back. But having brought her this far, he couldn't imagine doing that to Grace.

Without giving himself time to change his mind, he put the key in the lock and turned it quickly. He stuck his head just inside and called out, "Sophie?"

There was music coming from somewhere in the house and light shone from the upstairs hallway.

A bark sounded from the top of the stairs and then Grace's dog came scampering down the steps.

"Lily!" Grace said, clapping her hands together.

The dog's tail wagged so hard, it was a near blur.

Where was Sophie? Caleb's bad feeling intensified. "Grace, would you wait here with Lily while I look for your mama?"

The child nodded.

In the kitchen, Caleb opened a couple of cabinets, found some animal crackers and took them into the living room for Grace before heading upstairs.

Grace's bedroom was the first on the right, judging by the little-girl baby dolls and stuffed animals. He passed another that looked like a guest room. The door to the room at the end of the hall was closed. He knocked, tentatively, and then more forcefully.

He turned the knob. Not locked. He opened the door a few inches and called her name again. He stuck his head just inside and saw her on the bed. She lay with her face away from him, and there was something in the way she appeared to have collapsed into the position that sent a spear of panic through him.

"Sophie?" He crossed the rug-covered floor to the bed, his heart pounding hard. He put his hand on her shoulder, but she didn't move. Fear grabbed him by the throat now. She wouldn't do this. He scanned the room for signs of anything she might have taken, then ran to the bathroom, flicking on the light.

A bottle sat on the sink, the lid removed. He

picked up the container and quickly scanned the label. For Temporary Relief of Insomnia. Quantity: 8.

The bottle was empty. He dropped it into the sink as if it had scalded him. In the bedroom, he sat on the edge of the mattress and lifted her to a sitting position. "Sophie. Sophie, can you hear me?"

Her head lolled back and another hammer of panic slammed through him. This couldn't be happening. She wouldn't have done this. He grabbed her wrist, put his thumb to her pulse. Thank God, it was there.

Putting an arm under her legs, he picked her up and carried her into the bathroom. He opened the shower door, set her against the wall, then turned on the water, checking to make sure the temperature was right. He pointed the nozzle directly at her, the cold water sluicing across her face.

For a couple of moments there was no response, and then she made a sound, visibly struggling to open her eyes.

Within seconds, she was completely soaked, the cotton of her white blouse sticking to her skin and outlining the sheer bra beneath.

She made another sound of protest and opened her eyes fully, looking up at him. He could see her trying to focus, finally registering his presence.

"Oh, no," she said so softly he could barely hear her.

He turned off the shower. "Are you all right?"

She turned her head to the side and squeezed her eyes together. "Why are you here?"

Before he could answer, she jerked her gaze back to him and began struggling to get up. "Oh, my God. Grace. Is she all right?"

Caleb squatted down, placing his hands on her wet shoulders. "She's fine. Let's talk about you for a second."

She looked up at him, relief in her eyes. "Where is she?"

"Downstairs with Lily. How many of those pills did you take?"

Sophie sank back against the wall of the shower as if her bones refused to hold her up. "I'm not sure. I—" She thought for a moment and then said, "Oh. You don't think I tried to—"

"I don't know what to think."

"I just wanted to sleep for a while. I didn't think I could stand—" She stopped again, as if realizing he wasn't the one she should be telling this to.

"There were no pills in that bottle. How many did you take?"

She frowned. "I...a couple, I think. I just wanted to make it all go away for a little while."

The honesty of the words turned the blade of

remorse inside him several degrees. In trying to get his own life back to a place of sanity, how had he managed to block out the devastation he would be bringing to this woman's life, to Grace's life? Here, in this moment, he was sorry to see how successfully he had managed to ignore all but his own pain and the need to end it.

"Wait right here, okay?"

She nodded once and rubbed at her eyes.

He headed back downstairs to the living room where Grace was happily sharing her animal crackers with Lily. Caleb gave her a few more and then went to the kitchen, found the coffeepot on a counter, filled it halfway. He searched the pantry for coffee, finally thinking to look in the freezer where he found a bag of beans. He dumped some in the grinder beside the pot, measured out a few tablespoons, then poured in the water.

"Where's Mama?"

Grace stood in the doorway, her small voice surprising him. "She was asleep. I'm making her some coffee, and then she'll be right down."

Grace danced one of the animal crackers through the air, but otherwise didn't acknowledge what he'd said, as if she was considering whether to believe him. She turned and went back to the living room.

Once the coffee had finished, Caleb filled a cup and retraced his steps back upstairs.

Sophie still sat on the shower floor with her head resting against the tile wall. Her eyes were heavy, as if she could barely keep them open.

"Here," he said, squatting beside her and putting the cup to her lips.

She blinked once, sipped the hot coffee, then took the cup from him, touching the back of one hand to her mouth. "Thank you."

They said nothing for a few more sips. Halfway through the cup, she straightened her back against the wall and pushed her hair from her face. "Are you all right?" he asked.

"Better."

"Can you stand?"

She nodded, accepting his hand to help pull herself up. She managed to lean against the wall, then glanced down at the blouse clinging to her skin. She raised both arms to cover herself while awkwardness struck them both mute.

Caleb set his gaze on the shower floor and said, "If you'll tell me where to find them, I'll get you some dry clothes."

"Anything from the closet. Maybe just my robe."

He went into the bedroom, retrieved it from the hook on the closet door. When he returned to the bathroom, she looked as if it had required every ounce of her strength to remain standing.

"I didn't do this intentionally," she said.

He handed her the robe and turned his back to her. "It didn't seem in character."

"Meaning?"

"You seem like a strong woman," he said, unsettled by the rustling sound of clothing being removed.

"I'm not sure how you could think that considering my current state." She stepped around him to drop the wet clothes in a pile by the sink. Her hair still dripped water. She reached for a towel and rubbed at the ends. "Why did you bring her back?" she asked softly.

He didn't answer right away, and then admitted, "She needed to see you."

Sophie raised her gaze to his, and Caleb thought he'd never seen such gratitude—and he'd never felt so completely unworthy of it. Neither of them said anything else.

But then words didn't seem necessary when two people understood one another as the two of them now did.

CHAPTER FOURTEEN

DOWNSTAIRS, SOPHIE PUT a hand to her mouth at the sight of Grace patiently waiting on the living-room rug, arms outstretched, a smile lighting her face.

Sophie lifted her up, held her tightly and rocked side to side, breathing in the sweet child scent of her. Tears slid down Sophie's cheeks even as she tried to stop them.

"Don't cry, Mama," Grace said. "I'm back."

Sophie glanced at Caleb then. He stood at the edge of the kitchen, arms crossed at his chest, looking as if he wished he could disappear. "I'll be going now," he said.

A dozen different emotions assaulted her, none of which she had the presence of mind to separate and identify right now. She could only imagine what it must have cost him to bring Grace back today. "Thank you," she said. "Thank you."

Their gazes held for a moment before he nodded and left the kitchen, the front door closing quietly behind him.

WITH HIS DEPARTURE, the silence was stark. Sophie stood beside Grace, one hand on her small shoulder. Let him go. Wouldn't it be crazy to do anything else? But he had brought her daughter back.

She pressed a kiss to the top of Grace's head, ran to the foyer and swung the door open wide. "Caleb! Wait!"

He'd already begun backing out of the driveway. She ran down the brick walkway and stopped at his lowered window. "Stay for dinner," she said.

From the backseat, Noah stuck his head out and licked Sophie's hand.

"I should be going," Caleb said.

"Please."

He stared at her, then shook his head. "Look, Sophie. Don't make me out to be something I'm not. I brought Grace back because she obviously needed you. There's nothing selfless about that."

She considered the response, and then said, "I'm not trying to put a label on anything, Caleb. It's just dinner."

Another stretch of moments passed and his gaze held hers. He turned the truck off. She stepped back. He opened the door and got out.

"Noah's invited, too," she said.

Caleb lifted the seat. The dog barked and jumped out, tail wagging.

The three of them walked back to the house,

Noah leading the way. And all Sophie could think was how incredible it was that a single day could hold such surprises.

SHE PULLED INGREDIENTS from the refrigerator for a quick stir-fry. Zucchini, yellow squash, a couple of onions, sweet red pepper. The rice was already boiling, and she poured a little olive oil in a pan to sauté the vegetables.

She glanced out the window, her head pounding. Only this morning—could it have been that recent?—her world had gone pitch black, as if all the lights had been flipped out. Now Caleb and Grace were in the backyard throwing a Frisbee for Lily and Noah. Grace pointed at the swing set and said something while Caleb listened with quiet concentration.

He would have been a good father.

The thought tripped into her consciousness, bringing another realization along with it. Only a man with a good heart would have done what he had done today.

He had brought Grace home because he thought this was where she needed to be.

Sophie had no idea what it meant. She didn't want to think any further ahead than right now. Her daughter was home. And the man who had taken her away had brought her back.

THEY ATE AT THE KITCHEN table, Grace in her booster chair, Caleb at one end, Sophie at the other.

Caleb ate like a man who enjoyed his food. Sophie liked to cook, enjoyed experimenting with new dishes. His quietly issued compliments felt sincere, and it was nice to prepare something for someone who seemed to appreciate it so much.

Grace kept her gaze on Sophie for most of the meal, as if afraid she might disappear. When she yawned for the fifth time, Sophie finally stood and picked her up. Grace put her head on Sophie's shoulder, her small body heavy with sleepiness. "Bedtime, I think," Sophie said to Caleb. "Let me just take her upstairs."

"I'll go on home," he said. "You're probably tired, too."

"Wait," she said.

Several beats of silence ticked by before he nodded. "All right."

In Grace's room, Sophie changed her into pajamas, tucked the covers up around her and kissed her cheek.

"Mama, I won't have to go away again, will I?" she asked, snuggling into the pillow with Blanky clutched under one arm.

"Let's not think about any of that right now. Just sleep, baby, okay?"

But Grace didn't answer. Her eyes were already closed.

Downstairs, Caleb had cleared the table, rinsed the plates and put them in the dishwasher. "You didn't have to do that," Sophie said halfway across the kitchen.

He shrugged. "Least I could do for a dinner like that."

"Thank you," she said. "How about some coffee?"

"Sounds good. I'll check on those two dogs."

He went out the back door. Her hand shook a little as she prepared the coffee, and she told herself it had to be her body's reaction to a day of such intense highs and lows.

He was back in a couple of minutes. "Still playing. They've just about worn each other out."

Sophie smiled. "I'm sure Lily's loving it."

"Noah, too. I think he'll sleep for a week."

"Coffee's ready," Sophie said, a sudden spike of awkwardness forcing her to focus on pouring them each a cup. "Take anything in yours?"

"Straight up."

"Me, too." She handed him the steaming cup.

"Thanks," he said, gripping the sides with both hands.

She tipped her head toward the screened porch. "Drink it out there?"

He nodded and followed. Most of the back-yard was visible from the porch. Lily and Noah lay stretched out nose to nose in the cool grass, eyes closed.

Caleb smiled his rare smile. "He used to get like that as a puppy. Play until he was completely out of gas and just totally collapse. Laney said—" He stopped, then took a sip of his coffee.

"Go on," Sophie prompted softly.

He shook his head. "Nothing."

"Do you do that deliberately?"

"What?"

"Not talk about her."

"Probably."

"That seems like an injustice to her," Sophie said. "Especially when she must have been a special person."

Caleb kept his gaze on the yard, as if he was considering her words. Minutes passed.

When he spoke, his voice had the soft rasp of memory to it. "She used to say that the world would be a much happier place if people could feel the kind of joy for simple things that dogs do. If people showed their pleasure for seeing one another at the end of the day the way dogs do."

Sophie let the words settle, then said, "I think she was right. People make happiness way too complicated."

He tipped his head to one side, and she wasn't sure if he agreed or not.

"Tell me about her," Sophie said.

He turned his back to her and shoved his hands into his pockets. After a few moments, he began to talk, and this time it was as if his response were being pulled from him by something beyond his control. "She liked to read. Sometimes, she'd ride her horse out just far enough from the house to be away from the phone. The horse would graze, and she'd lose herself in a book for a couple of hours.

"She loved to swim, too. She was on the team in college. Her mama and daddy said the first time they ever put her in water, it was like she'd been born there. She just knew what to do."

Sophie blinked. "That's how Grace is."

Caleb looked at her.

The silence held for a while before he said, "She was a good person, not a saint by any means. But she thought about other people, cared if she said something unintentionally hurtful, couldn't rest until she'd set it right again. We started going out in high school. Neither of us ever dated anyone else. I knew the first time I saw her that she was the one."

He hesitated and then said, "It feels good to talk about her. Sometimes I wish I could erase it all. Even the good because remembering it makes not having her so painful."

Sophie reached out to touch his shoulder, the impulse immediate, if not well thought out. "You shouldn't blame yourself for what happened, Caleb."

Something she could only identify as anguish flickered across his face.

"It would be natural," she went on, "to look for a way to put reason into something that makes no sense at all. But sometimes there is no reason."

He was silent still, and Sophie began to wonder if she'd overstepped her bounds. Around them, darkness had settled, sounds carrying from neighboring yards. Children being called in for the night. Doors clicking closed. A cat voicing protest over invaded territory.

"I often wish the police hadn't shot him."

Caleb's voice startled her a little, and it took a second for the words to penetrate. She started to say something, anything, then stopped, sensing that what he needed was someone to listen.

"Sometimes, I wish he were in prison so I could go and see him locked up, ask him if he misses his life. I wish I could see him paying for what he did."

Bitterness colored the words, and Sophie thought what an awful burden that would be to carry the distance of a lifetime.

"What happened to him?" she asked quietly.

"He abducted another woman in South Carolina. Someone saw him shove her in the car and called the police. He held her hostage for most of a day before they took him out."

The picture was an ugly one, and Sophie shied from sketching in too many details. It didn't seem possible to connect this man with her daughter.

"When I look at Grace…she's such a perfect child," Caleb said, echoing her thoughts.

"I like to think that she got all of your wife's goodness. That it was her gift to Grace."

Caleb looked at her then, and even in the night shadows, she could see appreciation in his eyes. "I see so much of Laney in her."

"I'm glad," Sophie said. And she really was.

"Tell me about your family, Sophie." The request was quiet and direct with what sounded like sincere interest.

"There really isn't much to tell."

"Your aunt and uncle are your closest relatives?"

She nodded, old hurts rising up to mingle with far more recent ones. "And not that close, as you saw in court," she said, irony in her voice.

"Were they good to you when you were growing up?"

"I had a roof over my head," she said, hearing

the flatness in the words. "I suppose they felt ob-
ligated to take care of me when my parents and my
sister died."

"What happened to them?"

Caleb's gaze was intent on her, so much so that
she angled a shoulder away from him, afraid he
would see too much. "Our house burned down
one night. I was the only one who got out."

He drew in an audible breath. "I'm sorry."

"My aunt and uncle weren't able to have children of their own. I wasn't exactly what she
wanted. Kind of like a consolation prize."

Caleb put a hand on her shoulder. She jumped
at the touch. He turned her to face him, looking
into her eyes with an intensity that made her
glance away. "They should have been grateful to
have you, Sophie."

"They took care of me," she defended automatically as she always had. "I could have ended up
in foster care or worse."

She had never told any of her friends what she
had just told Caleb for fear that it would make her
a lesser person in their eyes. She had never even
told her ex-husband everything, rather a glossed-
over version of her childhood that didn't encour-
age too many questions.

They stood there for a while, neither of them
saying anything, or feeling compelled to do so.

She remembered suddenly the attraction she'd felt to him the first time she'd seen him, before the truth had come to light. She wanted to touch him. Wished he'd reach for her, put his mouth to hers.

She stepped away then, too quickly, and bumped her coffee cup from the end table where she had set it earlier.

It toppled onto the stone floor of the porch and broke.

"Oh, no," she said, dropping down to pick up the largest pieces.

"It didn't cut you, did it?" Caleb asked.

"No," she said.

He knelt beside her to help gather the rest of the shattered cup. "I think that's all of it."

The words clearly marked the moment for them to stand, move apart, dilute the sudden thickness of the air around them. But they stayed where they were, watching one another.

Most shocking was the look on Caleb's face, a reflection of the same longing that Sophie felt.

"Sophie," he said, his voice not sounding like his at all.

She couldn't speak, could find no words to answer the questions she heard in her name.

"I should go home," he said.

"It's late," she agreed, her gaze on her hands.

They both moved for the sliding door at the same

time, creating an awkward two-step where they avoided eyes and said simultaneous excuse-mes.

In the kitchen, she put the broken cup in the trash, made a pretense of washing her hands at the sink just so she could keep her back to him.

His boots sounded on the floor behind her. He touched her shoulder. "Sophie?"

She turned to look at him, not trusting herself to speak.

"You would regret it," he said.

"*I* would? Or you would?"

"Both of us, I suspect." He pulled his hand back as if her skin had suddenly become burning hot. He went to the back door and called Noah. The dog bolted up the steps, Lily trotting in behind him and coming over to sit at Sophie's feet.

"Thanks again for the dinner," he said.

"You're welcome."

"Good night, Sophie."

"Good night."

For a long time after the front door clicked quietly closed, she stood at the kitchen sink, rubbing Lily's soft head and trying to decide exactly what had just happened.

CHAPTER FIFTEEN

THE SHOT GLASS TAVERN had lived two lives in Albemarle County. The first was in an old log cabin just inside the town limits. When a fire had burned the place to the ground in 1978, the owners relocated to what had once been a tobacco warehouse farther out where it wasn't quite so handy for police cruisers to roll by looking for overindulged customers.

Caleb didn't realize he'd marked the place as his destination until he turned in at the metal entrance sign and shut off the truck's diesel engine. A dozen or so cars were scattered throughout the gravel parking lot. Two more pulled in behind him, radios blasting through rolled-down windows.

He hadn't been inside the bar in years. Happy, married people had no use for such a place. But tonight, it suited his purpose.

He lowered the windows a couple of inches and told the already sleeping Noah to wait there. He got out of the truck and hit the remote lock. From outside, thick concrete-block walls and a heavy front door muffled the bar noise. Inside, the blast hit from the speakers hanging in each corner of the ceiling with a row of them down the center, alternating directions. Clint Black held the current spot on the jukebox stage, and several couples danced groin to groin on the small wood floor at the far end of the bar.

Caleb took a stool and ordered a Jack Daniel's straight up.

The bartender dropped him a nod, reached for the bottle and poured the shot. Caleb upended the glass, drained the bourbon in a single gulp, then set it down for another. The bartender raised an eyebrow as he poured again.

Caleb blinked against the burn blazing down his throat and waited for the numbness to set in. It started with a slow tingle in the center of his belly, then washed out toward fingers and toes. Effective as the liquor was, it didn't change the fact that he'd wanted to kiss Sophie Owens tonight.

There.

Had he needed the bourbon to point that out?

For three years, that part of him had ceased to exist. Just wasn't there anymore. He'd pass an attractive woman on the street and feel nothing. He hadn't missed what he didn't want.

She had wanted him to kiss her. He'd felt that, too. And for a few clear seconds, he'd been tempted.

It scared the hell out of him.

He'd imagined that if those kinds of feelings ever came back, they would trickle in one at a time, until he woke up one day and decided it was time to act on them. In a planned, logical, fully aware of the consequences kind of way.

But not like this. Not in a gust of physical need that nearly knocked him off his feet. And not with Sophie Owens.

He didn't need to add to his list of offenses seducing a woman whose life he had already shaken off its foundation.

"Hey, there."

Caleb turned his head. A blond twenty-something studied him with a smile that went a few watts beyond friendly. "Hey," he said.

"You and Jack look like you could use some company."

"We were just leaving," Caleb said, tipping the edge of his now-empty glass.

"Oh, come on," she said, placing two fingers on his left arm. "It's way early. Things are just getting started." Her voice held a note of appeal, and her wide green eyes urged him to stay.

The crowd around them had indeed thickened,

and laughter rang out with the sound of people enjoying themselves.

He dropped his gaze to her hand, waiting for a spark of interest to flare beneath her touch.

None came.

Instead, all he felt was disappointment and an inexplicable urgency to prove that what had happened earlier tonight had been need in general and nothing specific to the one woman he could not get involved with.

"One dance," he said.

The girl's smile widened, her voice cigarette-husky when she said, "Great."

The dance floor had gotten more popular with the slowing of the music, and Caleb followed her to a corner where there was barely enough room for them to squeeze in. She stepped right up against him, looped her arms around his neck and tipped her head back with another inviting smile.

"My name's Megan," she said. "I'm a student at the university. And you're—"

"Too old for you," he said, looking down at her with an attempt at lightness.

"That's not exactly what I was thinking," she said with another smile. He suspected she knew how appealing it was. "I was thinking you're just about right. I haven't had a date on campus in the last year that I didn't wish would end by ten o'clock."

"Maybe you've been accepting the wrong dates."

"Maybe," she said. "Or maybe I just haven't run into the right man. Until now."

The last two words had deliberate emphasis, and Caleb knew he should at least feel a little flattered. Feel something, anyway. He focused on finding the rhythm in the song and noticed with a kind of removed-from-the-moment detachment the fact that their knees bumped as they danced, that her halter-covered breasts brushed his chest with every turn of their bodies.

"So what's your name?" she asked.

"Caleb Tucker," he said.

"Caleb," she repeated as if she liked the feel of it on her tongue. "What do you do for a living, Caleb?"

"Farm supply store—"

"Tucker's?"

He nodded.

"I love that place! Every spring I buy petunias and impatiens and geraniums for Mother's Day. My mom is big into flowers."

"Glad to hear it," Caleb said. She was young. And he suddenly felt a lot older than he had when he'd come into this place. Aside from that, the Jack Daniel's lift had already fizzled, leaving him with a dull headache in his left temple.

"I'll have to drop by and see you sometime."

Clearly embedded in the statement was the

hope that he would say something like "Do that," or "I'll be looking for you." She closed the distance between them by a couple more inches. And Caleb felt nothing.

The truth was impossible to deny. The desire he'd felt earlier tonight had been about Sophie Owens. Her touch. The clear hope in her eyes that he would kiss her.

The song came to an end.

"One more?" she asked with a smile.

"Time for me to go home," he said, already backing up. "Thanks for the dance, though."

"Wait!" she said, grabbing a book of matches from the bar, then asking the bartender for a pen. She scribbled something on the cover and handed it to him.

"Good night," he said and headed for his truck, fully aware that he never should have stopped in the first place.

THE DOORBELL PULLED SOPHIE from the tub at just after ten that night. Dressed in a robe and pajamas, she went downstairs to find Darcy on her front step, relief etched in her expression.

"I couldn't stand it another minute," she said. "I've been trying to get you all day. I was sure something had happened—"

"Oh, Darcy. I'm sorry," Sophie said, contrite. "You drove back to check on me?"

"It was either that or call the police."

Sophie waved her in, apologizing again. "I should have called you back."

They walked into the kitchen where Sophie poured them both a glass of iced tea and asked about Darcy's family.

"Everybody's okay," she said. "Gran was eighty-five. She had a good life. I'm trying to tell myself it's better to go the way she did, peacefully, in your sleep, than to linger for years not knowing your own children."

Sophie nodded. "Still. I've been an awful friend. Only thinking about myself."

"Hey," Darcy said. "You're allowed. Are you all right?"

"Yeah. I am. Grace is here. Upstairs asleep."

Darcy's eyes widened. "What?"

"Caleb brought her back this afternoon. He said she needed to see me, that she'd been crying since the social worker arrived with her."

"And what did he think she would do?" Darcy asked, bitterness edging her voice.

Sophie shook her head. "He was here for a long time. He ate dinner with us."

"You're kidding," Darcy said, disbelieving.

"I know. It sounds crazy. We talked. About his wife. Laney."

"And?"

"I think he's still trying to make sense of it all."

"While ruining your life in the process," Darcy said.

"That's what I thought. Before today."

Darcy looked at her for a long moment, eyes narrowed.

"What's going on, Soph? Are you falling for this guy?"

Sophie glanced up. "It's not like that."

"What's it like then?"

"I don't know," she said.

Darcy set her glass down on the counter. "My God. Sophie. Have you considered that maybe this is part of his plan? To make you feel sorry for him so you'll give him what he wants?"

Sophie heard the ugly suggestion behind the words and suddenly wondered if it could possibly be true. "I wanted him to stay. He's the one who left."

"Four years, and you have little to no interest in dating. And now him? That makes no sense, Sophie. You're the one who said the writing was on the wall when you were dating Peter. That your marriage was doomed from the start. Wouldn't Caleb Tucker fall under that same category?"

"Maybe," she said.

Darcy put a hand on her shoulder. "You've been through so much these past few weeks. Your emotions are on a roller coaster. Maybe you're mistaking gratitude for something else."

"Nothing happened. Nothing is going to happen."

Darcy was quiet for a few moments. "So what now?"

"The selfish part of me wants to go back to the way things were. Just me and Grace." She hesitated. "Another part of me wonders if there's a way to make this work for all of us."

"You mean share custody with him?"

"What if it's that or lose her altogether? I had a glimpse this morning of what that would be like. I can't let that happen."

"It's not right, though," Darcy said. "In every way that counts, Grace is your daughter."

"So here's the question then," Sophie said, holding her friend's concerned gaze. "If I willingly let him into her life, will that make her any less so?"

THE QUESTION STAYED with her throughout the next day.

Late Sunday afternoon, Sophie called her normal sitter and asked her to stay with Grace for a couple of hours.

She changed into khaki pants and a light blue blouse, deliberately choosing two of the most nondescript items in her closet. She pulled her hair back in a ponytail and slipped on flat leather sandals.

It was nearly eight-thirty by the time she reached the turnoff to Caleb's house. She stopped the car just outside the stone-column entrance, hands clenched on the steering wheel, her stomach doing multiple somersaults. A nearly choking sense of panic left beads of sweat on her forehead.

She eased the Volvo down the gravel road, reaching for courage as she parked beside Caleb's truck.

She saw him immediately, sitting outside on the front porch. Twilight draped the house in shadow.

She turned off the car, opened the door and got out. Music floated across the yard, the strains identifiable as Vivaldi.

The sound brought her up short, as if she were intruding on some private moment. "I'm sorry for not calling," she said. "Do you have a minute?"

He reached down and lowered the volume of the radio next to his chair. "Come on up."

She walked closer. "Please," she said. "Leave it on. It's nice."

He turned it back up, the soothing music drifting out over the evening. He held up a Corona bottle. "Could I get you a beer?"

Sophie started to refuse, then found herself saying, "I'd love one."

He got up, disappeared into the house, came back a minute later and handed her the ice-cold bottle, a slice of lime wedged in the top.

"Thank you."

"You're welcome. Sit down," he said, offering her the rocker he'd been sitting in.

"I'm fine right here," she said, dropping onto the porch's top step and taking a sip of the cold beer. "I wanted to thank you again. And apologize, as well."

He rubbed a thumb against his bottle. "No need for either."

"Yes, there is," Sophie said. "I wouldn't be honest if I didn't admit I'm still terrified by what you could do to my life."

"I must seem like a monster to you," he said quietly.

She shook her head. "At first, maybe. Not now."

He set his gaze on the far end of the yard. On the other side of the white board fence, cows grazed. "I wouldn't blame you for thinking it."

"Since you left Friday night, I've thought about everything over and over again. What happened to your wife is a tragedy, Caleb. What she left behind is a gift to be cherished. I have been blessed by the miracle of that gift. I'm human, and if I could wind back the clock to prevent you from ever seeing Grace, I probably would," she said, her voice lowering at the admission. "But I can't do that. And what I know is that I don't want to make this more of a tragedy than it has already been. If you want to know Grace, then I want you to know her."

Caleb stared at her, his eyes narrowing as if he couldn't quite take in what she'd just said.

"I thought maybe for the first couple of visits, I could be with her," Sophie added. "That it would make things easier."

He didn't say anything for a long time. And then he said, "That's incredibly generous of you, Sophie."

"Maybe more selfish than generous," she said. "I don't want to go through another day like Friday."

He let that stand.

"And about what happened before you left—"

"Nothing happened, Sophie."

"I know," she said. "But I just want you to know—"

"Sophie," he said softly, stopping her. "You don't need to justify anything with me."

She looked at him then, couldn't stop herself.

"For the first time in three years, I remembered what it felt like to want someone."

It wasn't what she'd expected him to say. She circled the top of her bottle with the tip of a finger, caught in a conflicting snare of attraction and sensibility. "I think we both know this is unwise."

"I would guess it is," he said.

She got up from the steps and set the bottle down on the porch. "Thanks for the beer, Caleb. I meant what I said. When you'd like to see Grace, just call."

And she left then while leaving was still possible.

CATHERINE LAY IN BED, the blinds in the room drawn so that only a slim ray of sunlight slipped through. She wasn't sure what day it was, two days or three, since she'd left Caleb's house. She'd started to call him a number of times, but it seemed to take so much more energy than she could summon even to reach for the phone.

She turned her face into the pillow, ran a hand across her sleep-flattened hair.

On the day the social worker had brought Grace to Caleb's house, Catherine had woken to an awful feeling of hopelessness. She'd managed to get herself out of bed that day and drive over there. But as soon as she'd left, the black cloud had begun to descend on her, and by the time she'd gotten home, it was all she could do to get upstairs to her room. She hadn't left it since.

She needed to get up. Needed to call Caleb and

see how things had gone. She regretted what she'd said to him, wanted to apologize. But her legs felt as though they had weights attached to them, and she could not force her body to respond to the request her brain was sending out.

The doorbell rang, the noise penetrating her thoughts as though it were coming from miles away. She tried to call out, tried to force herself to move, but she couldn't make her voice work. Fear lodged in her throat. A memory floated up from a place where it had been buried long ago. Her mother lying in bed for days on end. Catherine coming in each morning, trying to rouse her. "Please, Mama. Please, get up. I brought you breakfast. Can't you eat a little? Mama, why can't you get up? Mama, ge-e-et u-u-up!"

The sound of her own scream echoed in her head. She squeezed her eyes shut, tears leaking from the corners.

All those years when she had refused to compare herself to her mother, refused to believe that her mother's illness might have been something she couldn't prevent. She had just never wanted to be like her. Never wanted to be this woman lying in bed, unable to get up.

She heard the front door open, then footsteps on the stairs.

"Catherine?"

Jeb's voice. Oh, dear God. Jeb. She wanted to call out to him, and at the same time, disappear, so that he wouldn't find her here like this. See for himself that he had been right. But then, he *had* been right.

He appeared in the doorway, squinting against the dimness. "The car was in the driveway. When no one answered the door I got worried. It's the middle of the day," he said, frowning.

"What day is it?"

"Monday. Are you sick, Catherine?"

"Oh, Jeb," she said, her voice so weak she could barely make herself heard. "Please. Help me. Please, help me."

THEY WERE WORDS Jeb would have given any amount of money to hear from his wife these past three years. In reality, though, they struck terror in him. He'd never seen her like this, and waiting outside the hospital's emergency-room door, he struggled with the very real fear that he might lose her.

At the house, he'd carried her out to his truck and driven her to the hospital himself, unwilling to wait the twenty or thirty minutes it would have taken an ambulance to arrive. With every mile, the fear inside him had grown larger and more terrifying. And when they'd finally pulled up at the emergency-room doors, he'd been so grateful to see the faces of the doctors there, he could hardly breathe.

"Dad?"

Jeb turned to find Caleb walking down the corridor toward him. He'd called his son shortly after getting to the hospital.

"What's going on?" Caleb asked, stopping a few feet away, his expression drawn.

"Your mother," Jeb began, just as a young doctor came out of the emergency room and called his name.

Jeb stepped forward and said, "I'm her husband. How is she?"

"I'm Dr. Nelson. Could we sit for a moment, Mr. Tucker?"

Jeb followed the young woman to a group of chairs in a nearby waiting room, conscious of Caleb following them. "Doctor, this is my son, Caleb," he said. Caleb shook the woman's hand and they all sat.

"Your wife is severely dehydrated, Mr. Tucker. She says she's been unable to get out of bed for several days."

Jeb felt the color leave his face. "I— We've been living apart," he said, shame coursing through him.

"Has she been depressed before, Mr. Tucker?"

Jeb nodded, feeling Caleb's gaze on him, but unable to look at him. "Yes. But never to this extent."

"Has she sought treatment?"

"She would never agree to do so."

"I'm recommending that she be admitted," the doctor said. "One of our psychiatric doctors will meet with her in the morning. Hopefully, we can get your wife started on some medication that may help her. Meanwhile, we'll get some fluids in her and just make sure everything else seems okay."

Jeb stood and thanked her, before she turned and hurried back to the emergency room. Only then did he let himself look at his son, certain of the blame he would see in his eyes. And shocked to see something very different.

CHAPTER SIXTEEN

"I HAD NO IDEA." Caleb heard himself say the words, heard, too, their complete inadequacy.

"She didn't want you to know, son," Jeb said, his voice low.

"How long has this been happening?"

"She had a few episodes over the years, but in the past few, they've become more frequent."

"Since Laney died," Caleb said, a sick feeling washing over him.

Jeb didn't answer for a moment, and then he said, "Yes."

Caleb shook his head. "What a selfish bastard I've been."

Jeb put his hand on Caleb's shoulder. "Son. No one blames you for any of this."

"This is why you left. Why you couldn't support my efforts to bring Grace into our lives. Because you knew what it was doing to Mom."

Jeb shoved both hands in the pockets of his faded Levi's. "It was the coward's way out. I see that now. I love your mother. I never stopped loving her, even for a minute. She needs me. And from now on, I'll be there for her. No matter what."

Caleb walked over to a nearby window and stared out at the passing traffic for a long time before answering. "I'm sorry, Dad," he said finally. "Sorry I've refused to look outside my own misery. Sorry I couldn't see what was happening to the two of you."

"Caleb—"

"It's all right," he said, holding up a hand to stop his father from making excuses for him. He was tired of making excuses for himself, and he realized now how very self-centered he had been. "I don't want to stay in this same place, Dad. And the last thing I want is to hold either you or Mom here with me."

"Everything's going to be all right, son," Jeb said, his voice thick. His eyes bright with tears, he clapped Caleb on the shoulder. "Let's go see your mom."

Caleb nodded, and they walked side by side through the emergency room's swinging door.

LATER THAT AFTERNOON, Caleb pulled into his driveway and sat for a long time, staring at his house. He couldn't get the image of his mom in that hospital bed out of his head. He felt as if he'd been in some kind of dream state for years on end, each part of his body finally coming awake again.

He got out of the truck, opened the front door of the house and let Noah out. Ecstatic, the Lab flew down the steps, made three circles of the yard, before returning to the porch to lick Caleb's hand.

Caleb rubbed the underside of Noah's chin the way Noah liked, then went inside the house. He stood contemplating the stairs to his bedroom, not sure where he was headed until he sat down on Laney's side of the bed.

It was the first time he'd sat here since she'd been gone. He closed his eyes for a moment, then looked at the nightstand on which sat a lamp and the Bible she'd read every morning. He opened the top drawer, the red leather diary she'd written in each day just as she had left it.

He stared at it, then reached for it before he could change his mind.

He rubbed a thumb across the embossed lettering of her name in the red leather. Laney Scott. After they were married, she'd crossed out *Scott* and written in *Tucker* above it.

He'd considered looking at it countless times before now, but had never found the courage. He put one hand on the cover, slowly opening it to a random entry.

Dear Diary,

Caleb and I went Christmas shopping today.

We've been going out a little over six months now, and I feel like I should pinch myself every day just to make sure it's still real.

He bought me this really cool book on famous competition swimmers and what it took for them to make it to the Olympics.

He thinks I'm good enough to do that if I want. What a rush it is to have someone like Caleb believe in me. Swimming at the Olympics. Me. It's a fine dream, but the truth is I don't think I'll need anything that big to make me happy.

I have some dreams. I'd like to go to college. Be a teacher.

And then there's the dream where I'm married to Caleb, and we have this house full of little ones, Christmas and the other holidays bordering on out of control with all the racket and hoopla.

So back to the shopping. I found this cool backpack for Caleb. He loves to go hiking, and I love it when he takes me with him. It's so great being away from everyone else, just the two of us. It's as if the world is ours, and there's nothing we can do to screw it up.

That's what it's like when I'm with him.
I can be me. Just me. And he's fine with that.
Really fine. Maybe that's how I know what
we have is real.
xxoo
Laney

The words washed over him, but instead of the
anguish he'd expected to feel in reading them, he
knew an unexpected sense of comfort, the same
peace he'd felt those nights on the porch when
he'd either felt her presence or teetered on the
verge of losing his mind.

He flipped forward, stopping at another entry.

Dear Diary,
I think I weirded Caleb out tonight.

We went with our church youth group on
a day ski trip up to Canaan, West Virginia.
On the way home, we sat in the back of the
bus, cuddled up under a blanket because the
heater wasn't working.

Sometimes, we get off on these strange
discussions, like what we'll look like when
we're sixty-five, how it feels to skydive out
of an airplane, what happens after we die. Do
we go straight to heaven, or sit in some kind

of holding pattern while everyone else on earth gets a chance to make things right?

I think we go straight there unless there's something back here we still need to do. Caleb disagrees, though. He thinks once we're gone, we're gone, and if there's any work left to do, that's up to God.

I suspect He's pretty busy though, and I wonder if He expects us to help out with the hard stuff.

Caleb doesn't like to think about dying. It's scary stuff, I agree. But for me, it's all about knowing what you believe.

So here's the part that weirded him out. I don't think I'm going to live to be an old person. I've just always had this feeling that I would die young. No idea what that is. Young is relative, I guess. Anyway, it pretty much freaked him out that I could say such a thing, like I was tempting fate or something.

But then I finally figured out it wasn't the dying part that upset him. It was the thought that we might not be together. That he might have to live without me.

I suspect these are the kinds of words a person hopes to hear once in her lifetime. I wouldn't say this to Caleb, but I could die happy, now that he's said them to me.

xxoo

Laney

Tears streamed from his eyes. He didn't bother wiping them away, but let them fall across the pages, the words in the next entry so blurred he could barely read them.

Dear Diary,

So this sucks, still being in high school, being the one left behind.

I hate it.

Today was the day. Caleb's first day at college.

I went with his parents to drop him off and get him settled in.

It was so much worse than I ever imagined it would be. With every minute that passed, I could feel the divide between us growing wider and wider. Me still in high school, while he transitions to dorm life, keg parties and no parents to answer to.

The worst part was when we were getting ready to leave. There was this girl out front sitting on a bench with a book on her lap. She had dark hair with these incredible blue eyes.

I saw the way she looked at Caleb. Different from the girls who gawked at him in high school. Like he was the most amazing thing she'd ever seen, and she couldn't even meet eyes with him.

Driving away, I looked back, biting my lip to keep from crying. The girl got up from the bench, walked over and asked Caleb something. He smiled and pointed toward the dorm.

It was like I was already gone and could only watch them from somewhere really far away. Like he was already out of my reach, moving on.

But this was the weird thing. There was something a little comforting in seeing it, moving farther and farther away until they were a pinpoint, then nothing. And the sad part? I realized I could let go. If I had to.

xxoo

Laney

Caleb closed the diary, his heart throbbing. Like so many things he could not explain about his wife's death, he wondered if she had led him to these pages. If this was her way of telling him it was time. Somehow, he knew that she had, and with the acknowledgment came an instant wave of peace. The kind of peace he had not known once since losing her.

Grateful, he put the diary back in the drawer and slid it closed. He let her go. And somehow knew she was gone for good.

CHAPTER SEVENTEEN

THE REST OF THE WEEK FLEW BY. Sophie had two sets of essays to grade and a faculty meeting on Thursday. By Friday, she felt in need of a weekend. She picked Grace up from day care just after noon, then stopped by the grocery store. At the house, she unloaded the car while Grace played in the living room with Lily. The answering-machine light blinked. Sophie tapped the button and began putting the canned goods she'd bought in the pantry. The message began to play.

"It's Caleb." He paused and then said, "I noticed there's a new children's movie starting tonight. I wondered if you and Grace would like to go." He left his number and the machine clicked off.

She stood there, surprised. And yet, this was what she had suggested. She owed it to Caleb to do exactly what she had agreed to do. Act as the liaison that would allow Grace to get to know him without fear. She would keep her word.

THEY AGREED TO GO to the five-thirty showing to keep Grace from getting too off track with her bedtime.

The theater was half full, and they sat near the middle, Grace in between them.

Caleb had offered to pick them up, but Sophie had had an errand or two to do before and had said they would meet him there. They waited for him by the ticket counter, and at the sight of him, Grace wrapped her arms around Sophie's legs and clung to her. Sophie saw the flash of regret on Caleb's face, and she spoke softly to her daughter. "We're all going to the movie together," she said. "Caleb thought you might like it."

With that, Grace looked up at him beneath half-lowered lids and lessened her hold on Sophie's legs. "You'll be with us, Mama?"

"Yes, sweetie," she said.

Grace looked at Caleb. "What's it about?" she asked, her voice barely audible.

"A dog and cat who hitchhike across country to find the little boy they once belonged to," Caleb said.

Grace tugged at her lower lip with small white teeth, giving his response consideration. After a few moments, she said, "Okay."

Caleb insisted on paying. Sophie stood to the side while the usher tore their tickets. She tried not to notice how alarmingly good Caleb looked in crisp blue jeans and a white shirt. She was sure her smile looked as forced as it felt, and she reminded herself that this outing was about cultivating Grace's comfort level with Caleb and nothing else.

They'd taken their seats. Sophie and Grace shared a box of popcorn while Caleb had his own. The movie had its share of sad parts and, at one point, Grace wiped her cheeks with the back of her hand. By the end, Frisk the dog and Mimi the cat were reunited with Tommy, the boy they had been searching for.

On the way out of the theater, Grace took Sophie's hand and said, "I'm glad they found him, Mama."

Sophie nodded and said, "Me, too."

They stepped out into the early evening light, squinting after the darkness of the theater.

"There's an ice-cream shop just down the street," Caleb said. "Anybody up for some?"

"Me!" Grace said.

"Sounds good," Sophie agreed.

The shop was busy and they waited in line, studying the vast menu of choices. Grace decided on Rocky Road, while Sophie ordered pistachio and Caleb plain vanilla.

"Vanilla should be against the rules with all

those flavors to choose from," Sophie said once they were seated at a table in the corner.

Caleb held up his cone. "Doesn't get better than the basic stuff."

Sophie glanced away beneath the weight of his gaze, her face warming in a giveaway blush.

Grace licked at her cone with an appreciation bordering on reverence, while Caleb and Sophie watched, smiling.

"What was your favorite part of the movie?" he asked Grace.

She gave the question some thought. "When they're on the train, and Frisk saves Mimi from falling out the door."

"Mine, too," Caleb said.

Grace smiled and then giggled. "He had to walk on that skinny pole to get her."

They talked back and forth for several minutes, Grace's responses growing less wary, more natural. She smiled at him once and the effect of it was clear on Caleb's face.

They finished their ice cream, dropped their napkins in the trash can by the door and strolled back up the street to the lot where they'd parked. Grace was getting sleepy by now. Sophie picked her up and carried her the last couple of blocks.

At her car, Caleb took the key from her and opened the back door, stepping aside as she tucked Grace into the car seat. "Say thank you for the movie."

Grace looked up at him and said, "Thank you."

"You're welcome," Caleb said.

Sophie stepped back and closed the door. "Well," she said, folding her arms across her chest. "We'll be going then."

"Sophie?"

She turned, keeping her expression neutral.

He was silent for several long moments before saying, "I won't be calling again."

She looked at him, a feeling of unease settling over her. "I— What do you mean?"

He glanced down and kicked a booted toe against the asphalt. "I called my attorney today and asked her to drop my petition for custody."

"You what?" she asked, certain she had misheard him.

"I've let my own grief be my sole compass since Laney died. Somehow, I thought I could make things right with her by doing what I should have done when Grace was born. But sometimes, it really is too late."

Sophie stood there, stunned. This was the very last thing she had expected him to say. "Caleb—"

"I'm sorry," he said, backing away. "For all of it. I'm sorry."

SOPHIE DROVE HOME on autopilot.

She couldn't quite believe what had just happened, Caleb's words still swirling in her mind.

At home, she tucked Grace into bed, while the little girl talked about the movie they had seen. When Grace grew sleepy, Sophie said the prayer they said every night, then gave her daughter a kiss and left the room.

Downstairs, she called Darcy and asked if she could come over.

Darcy arrived twenty minutes later, wearing a jacket over her pajamas. "This could have been a little embarrassing had I gotten pulled over."

Sophie tried for a smile, but didn't quite make it. She poured Darcy a cup of the decaf she had just made, slid the cream and sugar across the table, then poured herself a cup.

"What is it, Soph?" Darcy asked, concern in her voice. "You look a little shell-shocked."

"I guess I am," Sophie admitted. "We went with Caleb to a movie tonight. He's dropped his petition for custody."

"What?"

"That's what he said. I'm not sure what to think."

Darcy jumped up, ran around the table and threw her arms around Sophie. "But that's wonderful! I can't believe it."

"Neither can I," Sophie said, subdued.

Darcy pulled back, giving her an assessing look. "Aren't you ecstatic?"

"I don't think it's really sunk in yet."

"What's that old saying? Don't look a gift horse in the mouth? *Why* doesn't really matter, does it? All that matters is that you have your daughter, and this nightmare is over."

Sophie nodded, taking a sip of her coffee. "You're right. It is all that matters."

"Sophie?"

"Hmm?"

"You're not feeling sorry for him, are you?"

Sophie shook her head. This much was true. Pity wasn't what she felt for Caleb. "No. It's just sad, you know. In the beginning, I wanted to see him as some bad guy trying to take away the child I love. But he's just a man, Darcy. A man who has lost more than I can begin to imagine."

"Don't go there, Sophie. You're not responsible for what's happened to him. You can't fix any of it."

Sophie laced both hands around her coffee mug. "You're right," she said. "I can't."

BUT FOR THE NEXT THREE WEEKS, the heavy feeling in Sophie's chest didn't lessen. The awful cloud of fear that had hung over her since the day Caleb Tucker had walked into her office and dropped a bomb in the middle of her life had finally lifted.

Food had regained its taste, the trees their color, the air its summer scent. And yet she couldn't stop thinking about him. Couldn't stop thinking about the fact that she could not pretend he didn't exist. Couldn't stop wondering what, if anything, she owed him.

One Wednesday morning, she sat in her office going over plans for a class she would be teaching in the fall. Life had resumed its previous rhythm, its familiar cadence comforting, and yet at the same time, she felt unsettled. With Caleb's entrance in her life, something had broken inside her, and now healing, it was as if the bones had not quite rejoined, refusing to fit where they had once been.

She should be happy. But a door had been opened. And try as she might, she couldn't seem to bring herself to close it.

CALEB EXPECTED THE DREAMS to come back, but they didn't.

He wasn't sure what to think of this, uncertain whether he had gotten it wrong when he'd let himself believe her tears had been about giving her child away. He chose to think now that he had. That she would be happy knowing that the child she had given birth to had a mother who loved her as Laney would have loved her.

For the first time in over three years, Caleb found himself getting up in the mornings with an interest in what the day would unfold. It started out as a trickle. He took a renewed interest in the store, made some changes in inventory that were long overdue, ordered new computers, even spoke to a Web designer about creating a Web site with the possibility of selling products online. At the farm, he made a long list of things that needed to be done, fences to mend, fields to fertilize in the fall, equipment to repair.

As the days passed, the trickle became a steady flow of energy, and he went at each of the tasks on his list with an intensity he had never imagined feeling again.

His dad came out and joined him every other day or so. They could talk again, as they once had, father and son. Caleb's mother was responding well to the medication she had agreed to try, and his father looked as if ten years had been lifted from him.

And, too, the work kept him from thinking. Kept him from wondering about Grace. And Sophie. Whether he would ever see them again.

AGAINST HER BEST FRIEND'S advice, Sophie called Caleb one Friday and asked if he would be willing to take Grace for a ride on one of his horses. Grace had been asking about learning how to ride a number of times in the past few weeks.

Sophie's call obviously caught him off guard. He was quiet for a few moments, his voice neutral when he finally said, "Sure. I'd be happy to."

Sophie hung up the phone, wondering if she was crazy for not leaving well enough alone. But now that the plan was made, it seemed right to her.

Sophie and Grace drove out to Caleb's one Saturday, the weather cool for August. Caleb met them at the front of the house, dressed in blue jeans and a navy polo-type shirt. Sophie's heart rate accelerated at the sight of him, and she realized, suddenly, how much she had missed him.

She unbuckled Grace from her car seat and lifted her out, then turned to look at him. "Hello."

"Hi," Caleb said.

The greetings were short and awkward, and any comfort level they had found with one another had disappeared. "How are you?" she asked.

"Good. And you?"

"Good," she said, noticing that something about him seemed different. He looked more relaxed, more…she searched for a word. Peaceful.

He dropped down on one knee in front of Grace. "Hey," he said. "I hear you're interested in learning how to ride."

Grace smiled and nodded. "Mama, too."

"Oh, really?" Caleb looked up at Sophie.

"Ah, I don't think that was in the plan."

"Oh, come on, Mama! You have to," Grace said, tugging on her arm. "Then we'll both know how."

Sophie looked at Caleb, wavering. "Do you have something really, really slow?"

"As a matter of fact," he said, a smile at the corners of his mouth, "I do."

SOPHIE'S EXPERIENCE with horses had been limited to the carousel kind. Or so she said. Watching her trot around the ring on Zach, his twenty-year-old quarter-horse gelding, Caleb wasn't sure he believed her. There wasn't an inch of space showing between her seat and the big western saddle, and she had the kind of straight-backed posture new riders often found hard to maintain since the natural inclination was to pitch slightly forward or backward in an effort to find balance.

Behind her, Grace ambled along on his mom's good-natured old mare, whom he'd ponied over behind Zach this morning for her to ride. Grace's smile would have lit a room, and something caved a little inside his chest at the sight of it.

Sophie passed the center of the ring where he stood. "Ready to try a lope?"

"A lope?" she called back, still sitting Zach's jostling trot.

"The next gear up."

Sophie looked doubtful. "Is it harder than this?"

"Easier, really. Like riding a rocking horse."

"Try it, Mama!" Grace cheered.

"You're doing great," Caleb said. "If you like that trot, you'll love his lope."

"All right," she said. "So how do I change gears?"

"Little pressure with your left leg only. Cueing him with the outside leg tells him which lead to pick up."

"Then what?"

"Just ride it."

Sophie trotted another half turn of the ring, looking as if she were gathering her courage.

"Outside leg?"

"Yep."

Zach responded as if she'd flipped a switch, easing into the lope as smooth as peanut butter. Sophie's laugh was infectious.

"Oh, my gosh! I'm loping!"

"Yaaay, Mama!" Grace yelled.

Caleb smiled. "Sure you've never done this before?"

"Oh, I'm sure," she called out. She did three circles around the ring and then said, "How do I stop?"

"Gently pull on the reins, then release the pressure and ask him to trot."

The horse did as she had requested.

"Same thing and now ask for the walk."

Zach made another perfect transition. Sophie looked down at him, open delight on her face. "That was incredible!"

"I'd say you're a natural."

She looked pleased by the assessment. "You're a good teacher."

"Nothing to it," he said.

She swung her leg over the saddle and dropped to the ground. Stiffness instantly infused her thighs, and she took a few cautious steps. "How long before I walk normally again?"

"Few days," he said, smiling.

"Can I lope?" Grace asked.

"If it's all right with your mama, I'll take you for a ride."

"Please, Mama?"

"Okay," Sophie said, looking less certain than she sounded.

"I'll need your mount, ma'am," Caleb said.

He took Zach's reins from Sophie and climbed into the saddle. "Could you hand her up?"

Sophie did so, and Caleb settled the little girl into the saddle in front of him. He held the reins in one hand and looped his other arm around Grace's waist. "I've got you," he said, "so just sit tight."

Grace nodded, and he urged the horse forward in a walk and then asked for the lope. They circled the ring four or five times, Grace's high-pitched giggles clear illustration of her pleasure. Caleb never let himself look directly at Sophie, although he was completely aware that her eyes never left them.

SOPHIE WATCHED THE TWO circle the ring, one hand pressed to her chest, struck by the picture they made, Caleb tall and strong, Grace small and protected in front of him.

"Mama, we loped!" Grace said when Caleb brought the horse to a stop beside Sophie.

"That was amazing," she said. And then added to Caleb, "You make it look so easy."

"It's like riding a bike. It is easy once you get the hang of it."

"Can we do it again?" Grace asked.

"That's probably enough for Zach since it's getting pretty hot out here," Caleb said. "He's got a good sweat going."

"Can we do it again soon?" she asked, still smiling.

"If your mama says so."

"We'll see," Sophie said, reaching out to lift her from the saddle.

They walked the horses back to the barn where Caleb gave them both a quick shower in the wash stall. He let Grace apply a few squirts with the water hose, and she was as happy as Sophie had ever seen her.

When they were done, they put the horses back in the pasture. Caleb turned to look at Sophie. "My mom and dad wondered if you'd like to come over for a cookout."

"Oh, well—"

"Only if you'd like to," he said. "Please don't feel pressured to say yes."

She glanced down, then looked up and met his gaze. "We'd like that."

They took his truck over to his parents' house. Catherine and Jeb were in the kitchen, assembling macaroni salad when they walked in. Sophie hovered in the doorway, feeling awkward. But Catherine waved her forward and put her to work slicing tomatoes while Grace went out back with Caleb and Jeb to get the grill started.

When the screen door closed behind them, Catherine looked at Sophie and said, "I'm so glad you could come."

"Thank you for having us."

Catherine went to the refrigerator, pulled out a head of lettuce, then rinsed it at the sink. They were silent for a few moments before she said, "I don't want to overstep my bounds, but there is something I'd like to say to you." She turned and met Sophie's gaze directly, her eyes moist with tears. "Thank you for what you're doing. You seem like a very kind person. And if anyone has been undeserving of pain, it's you and that beautiful little girl out there."

Sophie swallowed against a sudden wave of emotion. "Thank you." She hesitated and then said, "To be honest, at first I could not imagine sharing my daughter. But I know now that the story is so much bigger than just the piece that involves me."

Catherine reached over and squeezed Sophie's hand, brushing tears from her cheek with the other.

The back door opened and Caleb stepped inside, his presence filling the room. "Dad says we're ready for those burgers," he said, his smile fading as if he'd sensed the somber mood in the kitchen.

Catherine pulled a platter wrapped in plastic from the refrigerator and handed it to him. "Now be sure and tell him I said not to burn them. He likes to cook them until they look like shoe leather."

Caleb glanced at Sophie. "You two about ready to join us out here?"

"We'll be right there," Catherine said.

A few minutes later, they went out back where Caleb tossed a Nerf ball with Grace while Jeb watched over the burgers. They had put up a croquet set, and they all played a few fairly horrible examples of the game, Grace sharing Sophie's mallet. But the laughs engendered by their ineptness made up for their lack of skill, and by the time they were finished, Sophie's sides actually hurt.

The evening had cooled, an easy breeze softening the edge of what heat remained. It was the kind of casual, backyard gathering Sophie had heard described by many of her colleagues on Monday mornings, held often enough that they were taken for granted, sometimes even grumbled about. But it wasn't like that for Sophie. She yearned for family to call up and invite her over for a last-minute cookout or Sunday lunch. And so, while to Caleb, Catherine and Jeb, the evening might have been nothing too special, Sophie enjoyed herself and was glad she had decided to stay.

CHAPTER EIGHTEEN

AFTER DINNER, JEB and Catherine took Grace for a walk out to the fishpond, Noah and Lily happily leading the way.

Caleb and Sophie stayed behind, mainly because they weren't asked to go, and he had his own ideas about whether or not it had been intentional.

Sophie began gathering up the dishes.

"You don't have to do that," he said.

"I don't mind. I'd like to help."

He cleared the table, loading the dishes onto a tray. "If you'll get the door, I'll take these in."

She jogged ahead of him and held it open, then began loading the dishwasher. "Your mom and dad are great," she said.

"Yeah," he said. He told her then about his mother's illness and how it had been a turning point for all of them, especially him. "That was my wake-up call," he said. "I realized how incredibly selfish I'd been. That I had reached a point where I couldn't see anyone else's pain but my own."

"You were grieving. No one could blame you for that."

He turned the water off, pulled a Brillo pad from beneath the sink then stood motionless with it in his hand. "At first, it was that. Just blind grief. So dark I didn't think it could ever lift. And then later—" He hesitated, scrubbing at the edge of the pot, silent.

"Later, what?" she asked softly.

"I think I can see now that maybe I didn't want anyone else around me to be happy. If I could lose the woman I loved in the worst imaginable way, then how could it be okay for everyone else in my life to go on as if it never happened?"

Sophie put her hand on his arm and pressed once.

He looked at her then, their gazes locking. "I'm sorry, Sophie. Sorry for everything I've put you through." He brushed his thumb along the curve of her jaw. "You have no idea, do you?"

"About what?" Her voice did not sound like her own. It was soft at the edges like melting chocolate.

"You don't notice that men's eyes follow you. That they wish for the courage to approach you and most of the time don't find it."

She wasn't sure what to say. That it was not how she saw herself. She swallowed hard, the caring in his voice making her want to believe his words.

Caleb curved his hand to the back of her neck, then leaned in and brushed his lips against hers. There was question in his touch—*is this all right?* Something in the slight collapse of her body toward his or the sudden unevenness of her breathing said yes, and he kissed her again, really kissed her this time.

Her hands found their way up from the center of his chest and made a loop around his neck. His moved to her waist, guiding her more firmly against him so that they stood entwined in a lovers' embrace.

They kissed as if it were the only thing in the world that mattered. And suddenly Sophie realized how empty she had been, that some part of her had gone unfulfilled, unacknowledged for a very long time.

"Sophie."

She heard the contradictions in his voice.

She turned out of his arms, putting physical distance between them. "I should go. It's getting late."

Self-preservation had snapped walls into place. Deny before being denied. Leave before being left.

"Sophie, I—"

"Please, don't apologize," she said.

He put his hand on her shoulder, rubbed his thumb once across her collarbone. Sophie lifted her eyes to his. And terrifying though it was, it felt as if something began from that moment, like a seed popping from its nesting place in the ground, reaching out for light and air in its destiny to become something as yet unrecognizable.

CATHERINE AND JEB PUT the final touches on the kitchen and then went upstairs to get ready for bed.

She was in the bathroom smoothing night cream on her face when he came and stood in the doorway. "I know what you're thinking."

She looked up, their eyes meeting in the mirror. She started to deny it, then stopped. There was little she could hide from Jeb. "It was nice having them here, wasn't it?"

He crossed his arms over his chest. "Yes. But you've got to let the two of them figure this out, Cath. I don't want to see you get hopeful for something that might not happen."

"It would be nice though, wouldn't it?"

He came up behind her, put his arms around her waist and kissed the side of her neck. "I wish it could be that easy. But there's little in this world that's perfect."

About that, Catherine knew he was right. But still. "He smiled more tonight than I've seen him in years."

"I know," Jeb agreed.

They stood that way for a good bit, just holding one another, considering. After a while, they went to bed. Catherine turned to her husband, kissing him softly on the mouth. He kissed her in return, and she pulled him to her, loving him in this most simple and basic way, grateful to have back what she had nearly lost.

CALEB DROVE SOPHIE AND GRACE back to his house where they had left her car. Long after they'd pulled away, he sat outside on the porch, a dozen emotions weighing on him.

It was hard to know what to do with what had happened between them tonight. He'd wanted to kiss her, and so he had.

But nothing about the two of them made sense.

How could anything good come of a relationship with a beginning like theirs?

A shooting star flashed across the night-darkened sky. He'd never seen one on his own before. Laney had pointed one out to him once when they'd gone parking in the south pasture during a spring break from college.

"You can only see them if you let yourself look, Caleb."

Her voice echoed clearly in his head. And as if she had reached out from the heavens and handed it to him, he had his answer.

Nothing good could come of his relationship with Sophie.

Unless he let it.

SOPHIE SPENT THE ENTIRE next day trying not to think about Caleb. And so, he was all she could think about.

She relived every touch, every kiss until thoughts of them colored everything she did. There was nothing logical about her attraction to Caleb. And yet its hold on her was like some drug, altering the way everything looked and felt.

She gave herself a half dozen lectures, all centering around why it was a good thing Caleb had stopped.

And there was no denying the truth of them.

But not one of her pep talks prevented her from wondering what would have happened if he hadn't.

THERE MUST HAVE BEEN some reflection of those thoughts on her face that afternoon when Darcy knocked at her office door.

"You look different," she said, stepping inside and taking a chair.

Sophie closed the lid to her laptop. "Different how?"

"Like you have a secret," Darcy said, studying her.

She felt a flush spread across her cheeks, and busied herself with an entry in her Palm Pilot. "There is no secret," she said.

"You're blushing."

"I'm not."

"You are."

Sophie met Darcy's teasing gaze. And realized that she needed to talk. Maybe hearing herself voice aloud what had happened last night would illuminate the craziness of it clearly enough that she could stop thinking about it. "Caleb kissed me last night," she said, the words out before she had time to rethink them.

Darcy raised an eyebrow, but said nothing for a few moments. "So how was it?"

"Aren't you going to ask me if I've lost my mind?"

"Would it do any good?"

"The whole thing is insane," Sophie said. "It would never work."

Darcy shook her head. "I can't believe I'm the one saying this after everything I've said to dissuade you, but here's a fact. You look happy, Sophie. That should count for something, shouldn't it?"

SOPHIE GOT HOME FROM CLASS around four that afternoon. She spent an hour or so in the backyard with Grace on the play set. They had just gone inside so she could start dinner when the phone rang.

Sophie tucked the cordless under her chin and opened the refrigerator. "Hello."

"Sophie?"

At the sound of his voice, her heart dropped to the floor. "Hi."

"Hi."

A thousand different emotions were hidden in their reserved greetings.

"Do you have any plans tonight?"

"I was just starting dinner."

There was a moment's hesitation and then he said, "Would you like to come over? I thought maybe we could take a picnic out to this spot by the river. The sunsets are pretty incredible from there."

Sophie replayed all of the logical arguments she had put together throughout the day. Then rejected them all outright, and said, "Yes. I would like that very much."

SOPHIE HAD CALLED Becky Adams, one of her students who loved to stay with Grace whenever Sophie needed a sitter. She'd arrived with a bag full of books, and Grace had been so immersed in the first story that she'd barely noticed when Sophie had left.

Caleb was waiting on the porch when she

pulled up in front of the house. He looked glad to see her, a picnic basket in his left hand, a quilt hung over his right arm. They walked along the edge of a thick green hay field that went on as far as Sophie could see, winding toward the mountain in the distance. To their right were trees, mostly old hardwoods that had watched generations of landowners walk these fields.

"It's so beautiful here," she said.

Caleb stopped and looked out across the field. "I think so, too. For a long time, my dad thought about selling it. He's gotten a lot of pretty tempting offers over the years. But one thing he taught me was that owning land makes a person feel permanent, as if he belongs on that spot for the stretch of time he's here, anyway."

She looked at him, and something sealed between them, an understanding of sorts that neither of them could have imagined might come to exist a few months ago. To Sophie, it felt like something to hold on to, something rare and valuable she'd been lucky enough to stumble across.

They walked on and, after a couple of minutes, Caleb turned away from the green field and led her through the woods, down a winding path that found its end at the edge of a wide creek.

"We can eat here if it's all right with you," he said.

"It's perfect."

He dropped the quilt on a sandy patch of ground near the softly gurgling water.

It was a beautiful spot, the water so clear she could see the bottom, the rocks worn smooth and shiny. She wondered how many years it had taken to make them that way.

She slipped off her leather sandals and dipped her feet in. "Oooh, it's cold."

"It comes off the mountain."

She bent down, scooped up a handful and tossed it in the air, tipping her head back and letting it rain across her face.

Caleb stood just behind her. She heard him step forward, then felt his hand close round her shoulder. Sophie went completely still, suddenly terrified to look at him. She somehow knew that if she did, everything she felt would show in her eyes. That he would be able to see straight through to the core of her where all the feelings she'd tried to reason out of existence had taken root with no regard for her resistance.

"Sophie."

She turned and the moment was exactly as she had known it would be. She could no longer hide what she felt for him. She no longer wanted to.

He reached for her then, lifted her straight up against him so that her bare feet came off the ground.

He held her there, just looking at her, as if there were something in her worth taking time over.

Then he kissed her, quick and deep, as though he'd been thinking about it for a long time. As she had.

Around them, the creek trickled by, making its soft gurgle. The air held the heavy scent of honeysuckle, as sweet and potent as her attraction to Caleb.

They stood like that, locked into one another, kissing with the kind of hunger that demands satisfaction.

He put one hand at the back of her thigh. The air left her lungs in a whoosh.

He took a few steps backward, and they fell to the ground, landing on the blanket, laughing as they went. The laughter felt good.

They lay there for a moment, both a little winded, and then he rolled over, propping himself up on one elbow. He leaned in and started kissing her again. Sophie had never before wanted time to stand still, as she did now.

Then he pulled back, and with a gentle touch, brushed his hand across her hair. "Are you okay with this?"

She looked into his eyes. "Yes."

He kissed her again. And then again. His hand at the curve of her jaw, gentle but insistent.

She traced the line of his shoulder, the muscle there firm and contoured.

His hand went to the top button of her blouse, his thumb rubbing across the exposed skin. He unbuttoned the blouse, his mouth grazing the skin beneath with each one. He pushed the fabric aside and looked down at her with open appreciation. "You are beautiful."

And he made her feel that way. Maybe that was how people found one another. Recognizing someone who could make you feel like more than you were, filling the empty places that had never been filled before.

She met his direct gaze and said what was in her heart. "Here, with you, all the other stuff…circumstances…don't negate this. They don't have the power to dilute it."

"That's what I want," he said. "To let the rest of the world fade and just look at this for a while."

His eyes held hers for a string of moments that had no awkwardness, but rather the most basic kind of need and want. For the first time, Sophie let herself believe it. That there was something right and good in this. And that she deserved it.

After that, they didn't talk anymore. They didn't need to.

The sun had dropped, draping the creek bank in dappled shadows.

The picnic basket sat at the edge of the quilt.

And it was a very long time before either of them thought to open it.

CALEB LAY ON HIS BACK. Sophie lay with her cheek on his chest, the heavy thud of his heart in sync with her own.

They'd sat on the quilt eating grapes and homemade bread with a soft Havarti cheese. Drunk lemonade with chunks of fresh lemon. Full and satiated, they lay together now, staring up at the evening sky, Caleb holding her with a tenderness she had not expected.

"Caleb."

"I hope you're not going to say you're sorry about this," he said, his voice soft.

"You're not?"

"No. I'm not."

"What are you thinking?" she asked.

He didn't respond right away, and she found herself holding her breath for the answer. "That I feel happy," he said. "I haven't felt that in a long time. It's nice. Really nice. Just to feel happy."

She lifted her head, kissed the center of his chest, then put her cheek against him again.

They lay there, holding each other until the twilight began to flicker and give way to night. They got up, with obvious reluctance, dressed and gathered their things. Caleb took her hand in his and they walked back the way they'd come. And it wasn't until they got in sight of his house that he let it go.

SOPHIE THOUGHT ABOUT THAT the next day. And wondered if there was some significance to it. Then she told herself to keep the search for symbolism focused on her literature classes.

And still, it was there. This question with a needle at its tip.

What had happened between them—would it be anything more than a few hours when they'd turned their backs to the walls surrounding them? Or, now that they had stepped out into the light again, would the glare of reality wash away all the softness they'd found by the edge of that creek?

All the reasons why it could never work between them came hurtling back at her like some boomerang she had flung as far from last night as she could. It had taken its time turning back. But with its return came logic as clear as the mountain water that fed Caleb's creek.

Last night had been a gift. Something rare and special in its unexpectedness.

And maybe that was all it could be.

CHAPTER NINETEEN

BUT THEN CALEB CALLED that night.

Late. After she'd turned off the lamp beside her bed and spent an hour staring at the darkness above her.

She answered, her heart thudding.

"Hi."

"Hi."

"Hope I didn't wake you."

"No. I…couldn't sleep."

"Me, either."

Sophie rolled over on her side, tucking the phone tight against her ear.

"I know you're probably having a thousand doubts," he said. "But all I know right now is I want to see you again. I've spent the day coming at this thing from all angles, and I can't see what you and I are doing wrong."

A car drove down the street, the headlights flitting through Sophie's bedroom window.

"At first, it felt wrong," he said. "That I might

be happy. And I guess it seemed especially wrong that it might be with you. As if it would take something away from what happened to Laney."

He paused and then said, "But she wasn't like that. She would look for the positive in a situation. Figure out how to make that the end result."

Sophie sat up against her pillow.

"So," he went on, before she could find anything to say, "I was wondering if I could take you and Grace to dinner tomorrow night."

"Tomorrow night," she said. "That would be nice."

"Okay, then. It's a date."

"It's a date."

They were both quiet for a moment, as if absorbing all that had just been said and the implications of it.

"I'll pick you up at six," he said finally.

"We'll be ready."

THEY WENT OUT THAT NIGHT. And the next.

They took Grace, and it was scary how quickly it began to feel normal. The three of them.

Both nights, Caleb helped put Grace to bed, and they came back downstairs, sat outside and talked. About everything. Big stuff. Little stuff. Just talked.

And then there was the kissing. They did

plenty of that. To the point that it was painful not to do more.

But they didn't.

By some unspoken consent, they made out like teenagers, and then he went home.

They went out every night for a week, twice without Grace. Once to a movie and the other time to a low-key restaurant forty-five minutes outside of Charlottesville that had become a find for gourmets in the know. The food was wonderful, wall sconces throwing soft light across the tables, the scent of garlic and rosemary drifting from the kitchen.

Sometimes, Sophie felt she might blink and it would all disappear. She was happy with whatever it was they had. She didn't put a label on it, wouldn't have known what to call it had she allowed herself to do so.

But there were a few nights, after all the lights were out, when one question refused to be silenced.

How long could it last?

THE ANSWER MADE ITSELF known the following Saturday.

There was a new place just off Highway 29, home-style cooking in an old renovated log cabin. It had become popular with locals since it had opened in late spring. Caleb had been told they made a great cherry pie, and Grace loved cherry pie.

They'd finished their dinner and were waiting for dessert. Caleb and Grace were playing tic-tac-toe with crayons on the paper tablecloth when a woman came over to their table, a reluctant-looking man standing behind her.

"Hello," Sophie said, smiling under the assumption that Caleb must know her.

"You truly have no shame, do you?" the woman said.

Caleb looked up, putting the crayon in his hand on the table. "Mary. This isn't the place."

"But it *is* a place for you to flaunt your disrespect for my daughter?"

Caleb stood, the movement quiet and steady. He put one hand on Sophie's shoulder, the other on Grace's. "Don't do this, Mary. You're about to hurt the wrong people."

"You're the one doing the hurting, Caleb. How could you have anything to do with that child, knowing where she came from? How could you do that to Laney?"

Sophie gasped, pushed back her chair and stepped behind Caleb to grab Grace up in her arms. She all but ran from the restaurant, not stopping until they had reached Caleb's truck.

Grace cried into her shoulder.

"Shh, honey. It's okay." Sophie smoothed the child's hair. "Everything is okay."

"That woman scared me," Grace said, her voice shaking. "Who is she?"

"Someone who's not very happy, baby."

Sophie walked Grace across the pavement, rubbing her back until her crying softened to sniffles.

Caleb came out, stood next to them, his face set in merging lines of pain and anger. "I'm sorry," he said.

She looked up at him, wiping her hand across one eye. "Take us home, Caleb," she said. "Please. Just take us home."

Grace was asleep.

Caleb waited downstairs for Sophie to return. He stood in the middle of the living room feeling like a man who'd just had his world blown apart. The pieces lay all around them and he didn't even know how to begin to pick them up.

He heard her come down the stairs. She stopped just inside the doorway.

"What do I say?" She shook her head. "How do I explain to Grace what that was about?"

"I'm sorry," he said. And he was. So sorry.

"Grace is only three. How could she have said those things to her?" Sophie's voice broke.

Caleb crossed the floor and pulled her into his arms. "I never intended for either of you to be hurt like this. Even at the beginning of the custody stuff when I didn't know you, I didn't want to cause anyone pain. But now…I can't do this to you. To Grace."

He dropped his hands to his sides even as he wanted to pull her into his arms.

Tears ran down Sophie's face, her eyes a well of misery.

With that image searing his heart, he walked out the front door and forced himself not to look back.

SHE STOOD AT THE WINDOW, watching Caleb pull away.

She thought about the walk back from the creek the night they'd made love, the moment they'd come in sight of his house and he'd let go of her hand. Maybe he'd known all along that it would never work.

She climbed the stairs and went into Grace's room. She stood there for a few moments, taking in the child's sweet innocence. She carried Grace into her own room and got into bed. Grace stirred in her arms, made a soft snuffling noise and curled closer.

Sophie lay there, wide awake, holding her daughter until the sun rose.

CALEB COULDN'T SLEEP.

He sat up in one of the living-room chairs, replaying everything that had happened in that restaurant. Regret settled like acid in his stomach for the pain he had caused Sophie and Grace.

He wished for some way to rewind things, stop Mary from having said those awful things in front of them.

But it would remain in their memory like a permanent fingerprint. And he was responsible.

He had once been willing to let himself settle into the mire of what might have been. But he knew now there was nothing down that road but bitterness and anger. This was the road Laney's mother had chosen, and he felt sorry for her.

Not so long ago, Caleb had felt what Mary felt. He knew the power of that kind of anger, its ability to eat a hole inside every effort he'd made to move on with his life.

And that was exactly what he wanted to do now.

Move on with his life.

But first, there was something he had to do.

IT WAS EARLY MORNING when Caleb pulled into the Scotts' driveway.

Leo, the family's ancient beagle, lay on the front porch. He got to his feet at Caleb's arrival, gave a token rusty bark, then lay back down, dropping his head on his paws. He watched Caleb get out of the truck, thumping his tail in recognition.

Caleb climbed the steps, rubbed the old dog under the chin, then knocked on the door.

Emmitt Scott answered. "Come on in, Caleb," he said, as if he'd been expecting him. They shook hands and Caleb felt apology in the other man's grip.

Caleb followed Emmitt through the foyer and into the living room. Pictures of Laney were everywhere, like a shrine, and Caleb thought how this was not what she would have wanted for her mother and father.

Heels sounded on the hardwood floor of the hallway, and Mary came into the living room, an apron tied around her waist. Her face was set, her voice clipped when she said, "What are you doing here, Caleb?"

"I think we need to talk, Mary. That maybe we've needed to talk for a long time."

Emmitt left the room, making it clear that this was between Caleb and Mary.

Once he'd gone, Caleb said quietly, "I lost my wife. And I've grieved for her in my own way, Mary. My way. Not yours. You think because our ways are different that mine hasn't been as sincere or as respectful."

Mary's face reddened. "I never said—"

"You didn't have to say," he interrupted. "It's pretty clear. I would do anything to change what happened to Laney. Anything. But I can't go back and redo that day. All I can do is go on from here."

Mary held his gaze for several long moments, then glanced down at her hands.

"I believe I was wrong to give her child away," Caleb went on. "What I did was selfish. For me, not her. I can't change that, either. Grace has a wonderful, generous mother who is willing to let me have a place in her daughter's life. I'm grateful for that because it's what I think Laney would have wanted. There's so much of Laney in her, Mary. And that's what I see when I look at her. If you would let yourself, you might see it, too."

Mary stared at him. "And the child's mother? What is she going to be to you?"

The questions were blunt, and Caleb could see the hurt in Mary's eyes. She'd had more than enough pain in her life and he didn't want to add more. But he also needed to be honest. "Whatever she wants to be," he said softly.

Caleb left the house then and drove back down

the gravel road. He had done what he could. Mary could change. Let go of all the anger that held her prisoner. Or not. And if she didn't, it would be her loss.

THE CAR HAD BEEN PACKED since eight. Sophie couldn't spend the day wondering if and when she would ever see or hear from Caleb again. And so she had decided to take Grace out to Carson Lake. Grace was so excited, she'd barely eaten her breakfast.

The doorbell rang and Grace jumped down from the kitchen chair. "I'll get it, Mama."

She ran to the foyer, calling back, "It's Caleb!"

Sophie walked into the foyer, forcing calm into her composure and step.

Caleb stood framed in the doorway, holding a smiling Grace.

"Looks like I've come at a bad time."

There was something different in his voice, in the way he held Grace with a natural affection that twisted Sophie's heart. "We were going to the lake," she said.

"That sounds fun," he said.

"Mama, Caleb can go with us!" Grace said, clapping her hands together.

"I'd like to go," Caleb said. "Could we please talk first, Sophie?"

She could manage to say nothing more than, "Of course."

"Let's go out back."

Outside, he set Grace up in her sandbox, Lily supervising from the nearby grass. He walked over to where Sophie stood on the stone patio, taking her hand and leading her to the teak bench, where they both sat down.

"I'm not sure where I should start," he said, meeting her gaze full-on. "I feel like I've lived the last three years of my life in a fog, and I couldn't see an inch past what was right in front of my face. But I didn't care, because I didn't want to know what was out there. You and Grace changed that for me. And I don't want to go back to that place again."

The words pulled at something painful inside her, something she'd been holding tightly like a clenched fist, but now it began to loosen and unravel. She couldn't look at him.

He reached out to turn her face to him. "I'm sorry for everything Mary said, sorrier than I can ever say that you and Grace were hurt by that."

"We can't change what other people think, Caleb," she said. "I learned that a long time ago from my aunt. She always saw the glass as half empty. Refused to look for the good in anything. That's who she was. She resented having to take care of me after my parents died. And there were times when her bitterness made me feel there was something wrong with me. After a lifetime of feeling guilty, I've finally realized I did nothing wrong. I was just a child who needed a family. And the same is true for Grace. I won't let her grow up feeling there's something wrong with her. I won't."

Caleb was silent for a moment. "Terrible things happen in this world. Things we never see coming, things that change us forever. I have to believe, though, that there is good to be found. Grace is proof of that. That sometimes good can come from the worst times in our lives."

The conviction in his voice threaded its way through her heart. She was filled with the sudden knowledge that she and Caleb understood one another. Had traveled these last three years to arrive at the same place. Forever changed by a little girl whose existence they both chose to see as a blessing.

"And us." He stroked her hair. "This is good, too, Sophie. This is good."

She looked up at him, the words like a balm, soothing the pain of what had happened last night. Sophie thought of Laney, of the awful thing that had happened to her. That tragedy had brought Grace into this world. She thought, too, of her own fear of losing Grace and of how their lives had become inextricably entwined with Caleb's. Of how full her life felt with him in it. To be sure, there would be hard things to explain to Grace someday. Painful things. Sophie could only trust that when her daughter's questions came, as they surely would, God would provide her with the answers to give Grace peace.

"Sophie, I want you and Grace in my life," Caleb said now. "In whatever way I can have you."

There *was* good to be found. As Caleb had said, even in the cruelest of life's blows. Maybe a person could let the bad things be the final outcome. Or maybe they could choose to see the good. This was the choice he had made. It was going to be her choice, as well.

"Caleb," she said, everything she felt coming through in that single utterance of his name.

He reached for her then. She let herself be folded into his embrace, pressed her face to his chest and knew that this was where she was supposed to be. This had been the destination at the end of the long, curving road that had brought the two of them together.

It was a beginning. Or maybe a middle. Either way, a gift.